EOD SOLDIERS

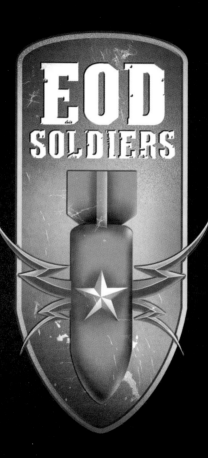

EOD Soldiers is published by Stone Arch Books,
A Capstone Imprint
1710 Roe Crest Drive
North Mankato, Minnesota 56003
www.mycapstone.com

Text and illustrations © 2017 Stone Arch Books

Library of Congress Cataloging-in-Publication Data is
available on the Library of Congress website.

ISBN: 978-1-4965-3107-0 (library binding)
ISBN: 978-1-4965-3111-7 (eBook PDF)

Summary: Private Eli Recato's fellow soldiers call him
"Bloodhound," but Eli isn't fond of the nickname. He isn't
fond of his self-appointed best buddy, Private Badger,
either. What he IS fond of is saving lives by sniffing out
IEDs in Afghanistan and disabling them. But when a bomb
finds HIM, Eli is faced with a difficult choice: hide with an
Afghan man he's never met before, or hightail it out of
insurgent territory without a weapon.

Designer: Brann Garvey

Printed and bound in the USA.
009620F16

TWO SIDES

written by Matthew K. Manning
art by Carlos Furuzono and Dijjo Lima

STONE ARCH BOOKS
a capstone imprint

EOD
SOLDIERS

"Initial success or total failure." That's the motto of the U.S. Army's Explosive Ordnance Disposal (EOD) soldiers, aka the bomb squad. These highly specialized individuals are the Army's top explosives experts. They have the technology, combat training, and nerves of steel necessary to locate and disable improvised explosive devices (IEDs) in even the worst of circumstances.

PRIVATE ELI RECATO:

Eli Recato is a private of Filipino descent who grew up in the Midwest. As his rank indicates, Recato is a pretty fresh face to combat.

PRIVATE TOMMY BADGER:

Badger is a quintessential
all-American type, but has a
chip on his shoulder the size of
a conjoined twin.

LIEUTENANT (LT) BRANCH:

As the commanding officer
of their road-clearing crew,
Branch is a tough leader with
an even tougher demeanor.

THE ROBED MAN:

The robed man is a
middle-aged Afghan.
His name is unknown.

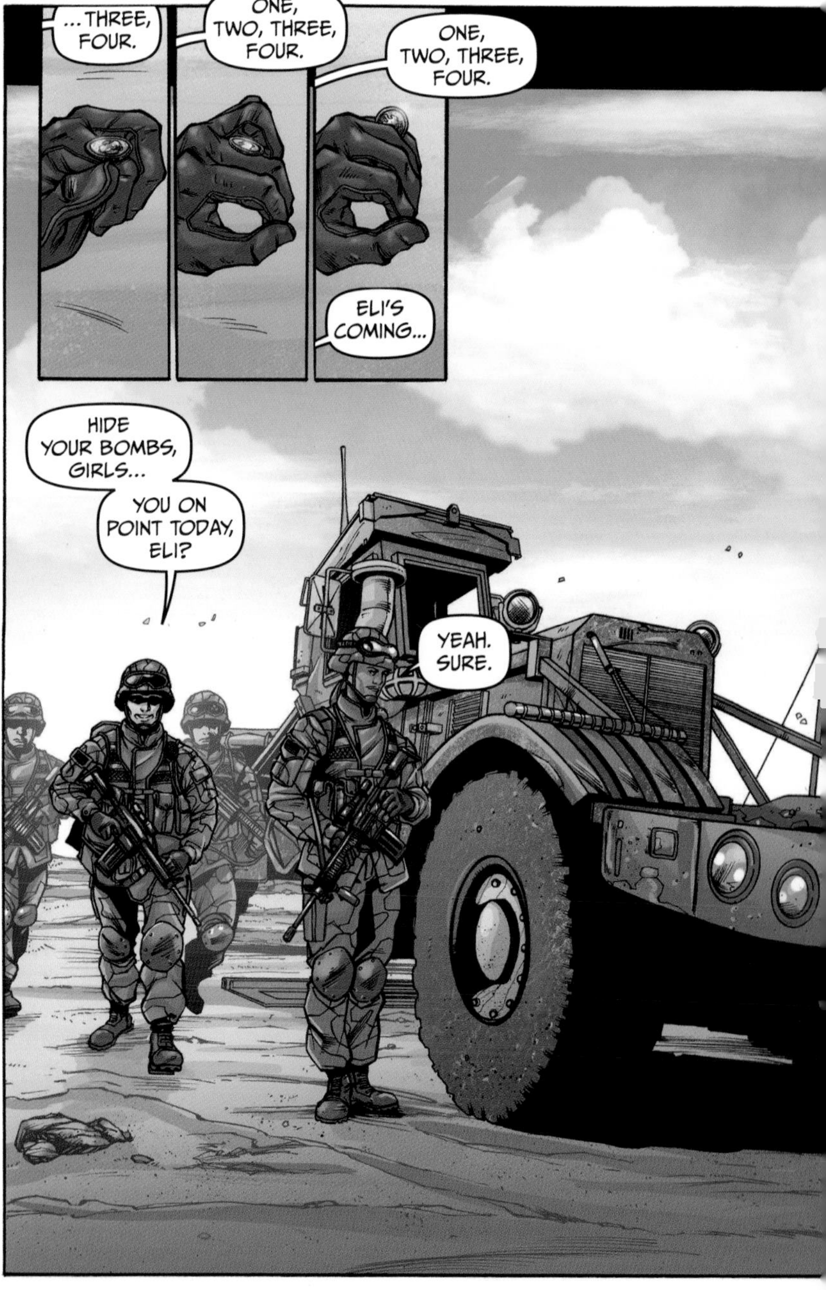
...THREE, FOUR.
ONE, TWO, THREE, FOUR.
ONE, TWO, THREE, FOUR.
ELI'S COMING...
HIDE YOUR BOMBS, GIRLS...
YOU ON POINT TODAY, ELI?
YEAH. SURE.

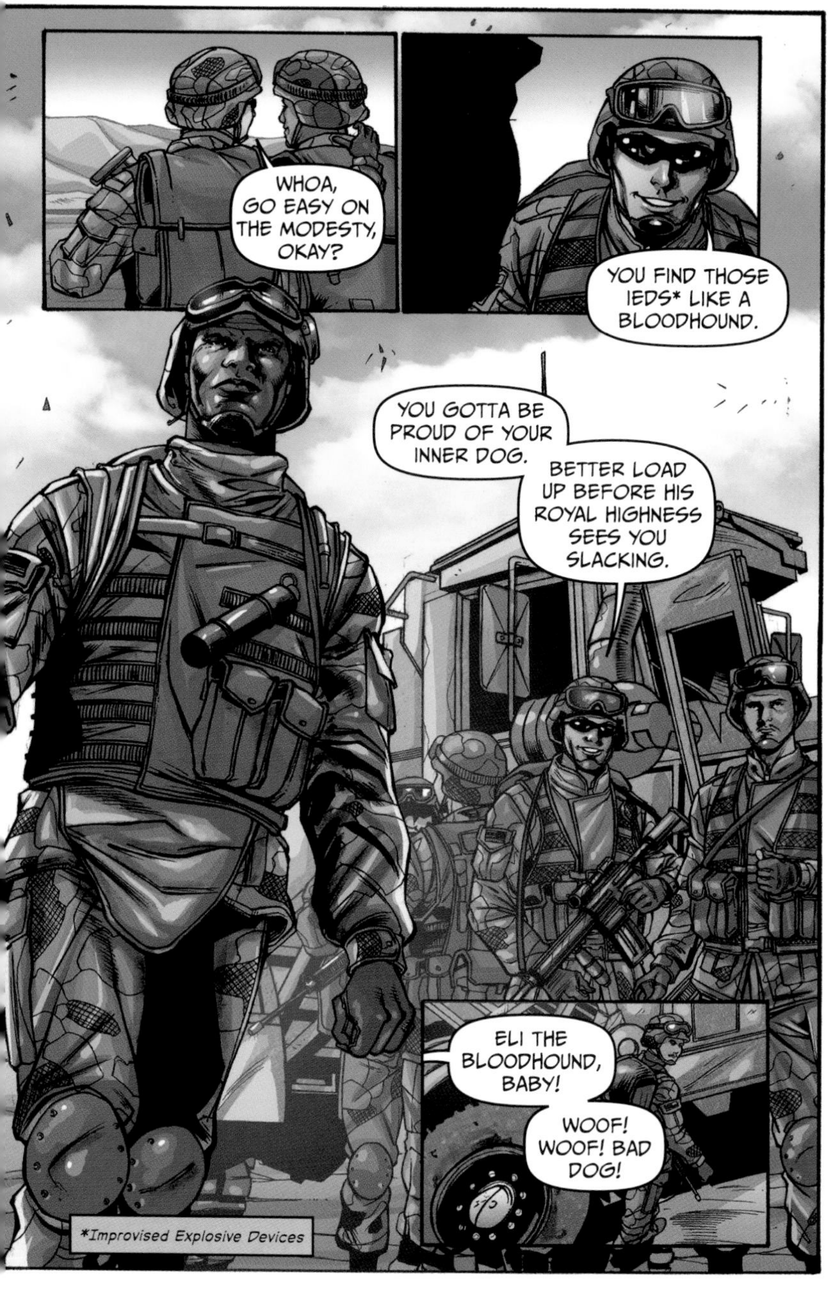
WHOA, GO EASY ON THE MODESTY, OKAY?
YOU FIND THOSE IEDS* LIKE A BLOODHOUND.
YOU GOTTA BE PROUD OF YOUR INNER DOG.
BETTER LOAD UP BEFORE HIS ROYAL HIGHNESS SEES YOU SLACKING.
ELI THE BLOODHOUND, BABY!
WOOF! WOOF! BAD DOG!
*Improvised Explosive Devices

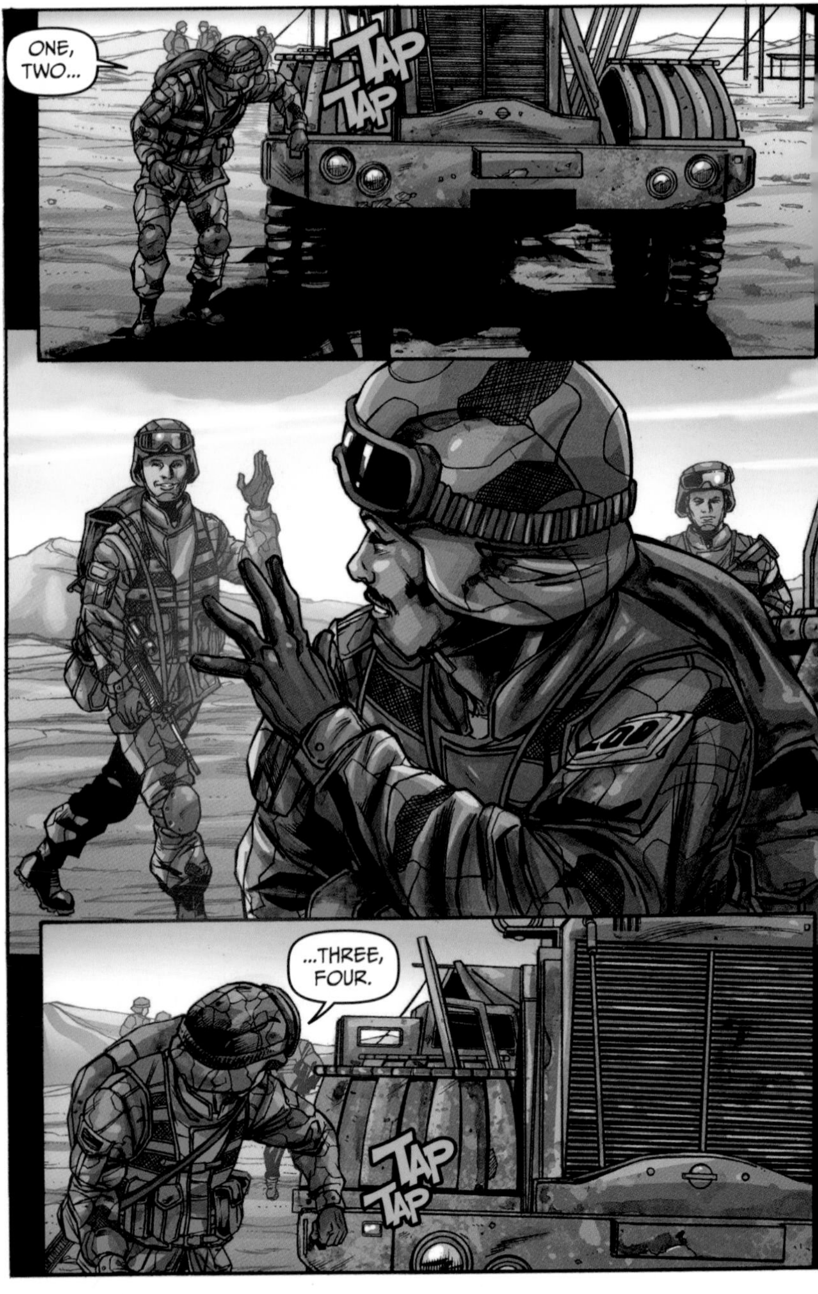
ONE, TWO...
TAP TAP
...THREE, FOUR.
TAP TAP

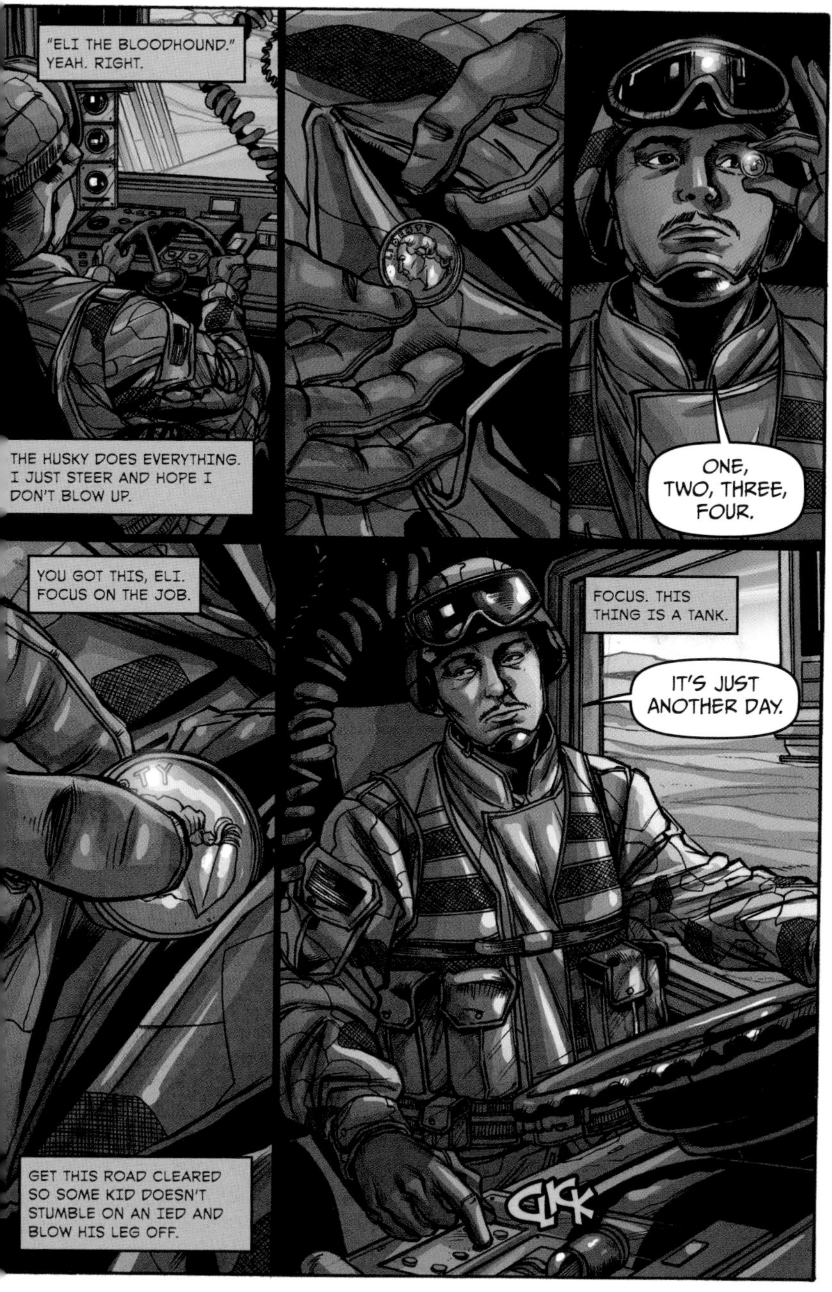
"ELI THE BLOODHOUND." YEAH. RIGHT.
THE HUSKY DOES EVERYTHING. I JUST STEER AND HOPE I DON'T BLOW UP.
ONE, TWO, THREE, FOUR.
YOU GOT THIS, ELI. FOCUS ON THE JOB.
GET THIS ROAD CLEARED SO SOME KID DOESN'T STUMBLE ON AN IED AND BLOW HIS LEG OFF.
FOCUS. THIS THING IS A TANK.
IT'S JUST ANOTHER DAY.
CLICK

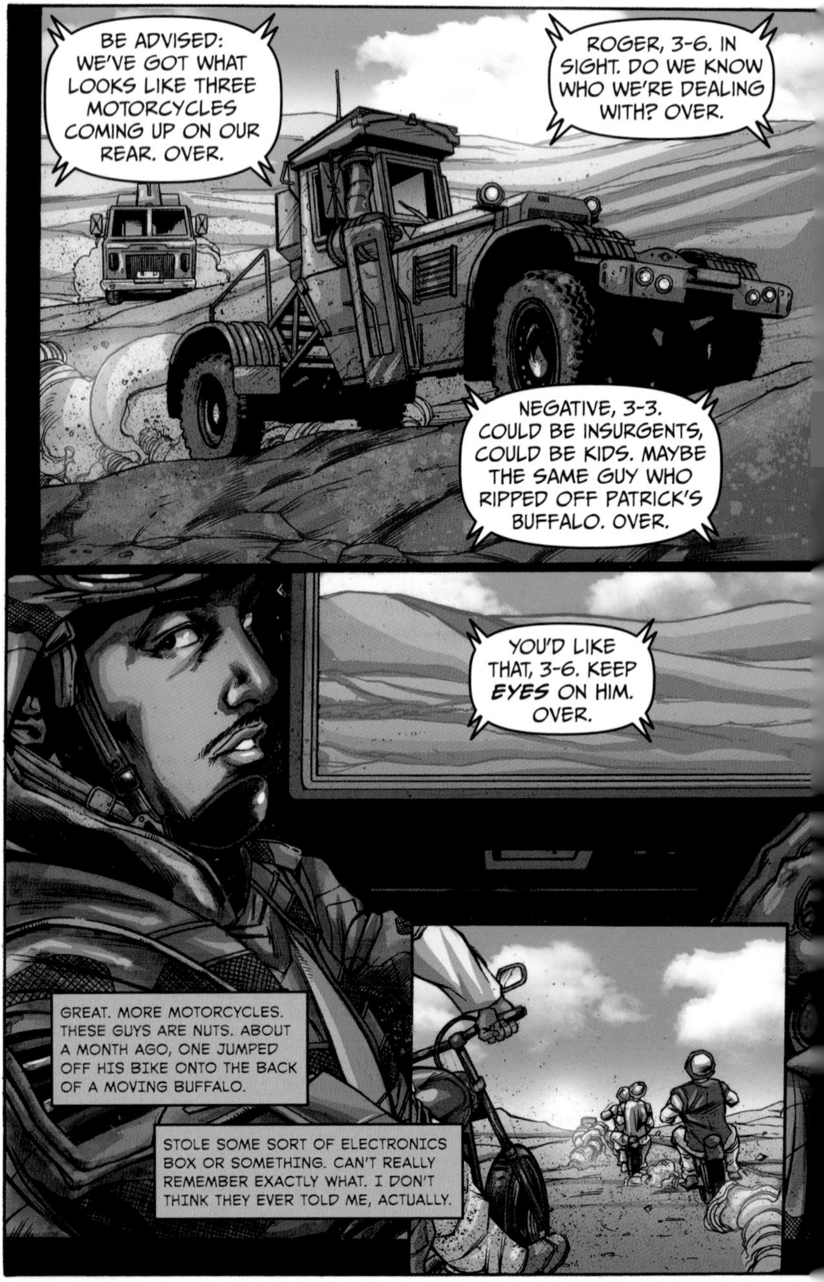
BE ADVISED: WE'VE GOT WHAT LOOKS LIKE THREE MOTORCYCLES COMING UP ON OUR REAR. OVER.
ROGER, 3-6. IN SIGHT. DO WE KNOW WHO WE'RE DEALING WITH? OVER.
NEGATIVE, 3-3. COULD BE INSURGENTS, COULD BE KIDS. MAYBE THE SAME GUY WHO RIPPED OFF PATRICK'S BUFFALO. OVER.
YOU'D LIKE THAT, 3-6. KEEP *EYES* ON HIM. OVER.
GREAT. MORE MOTORCYCLES. THESE GUYS ARE NUTS. ABOUT A MONTH AGO, ONE JUMPED OFF HIS BIKE ONTO THE BACK OF A MOVING BUFFALO.
STOLE SOME SORT OF ELECTRONICS BOX OR SOMETHING. CAN'T REALLY REMEMBER EXACTLY WHAT. I DON'T THINK THEY EVER TOLD ME, ACTUALLY.

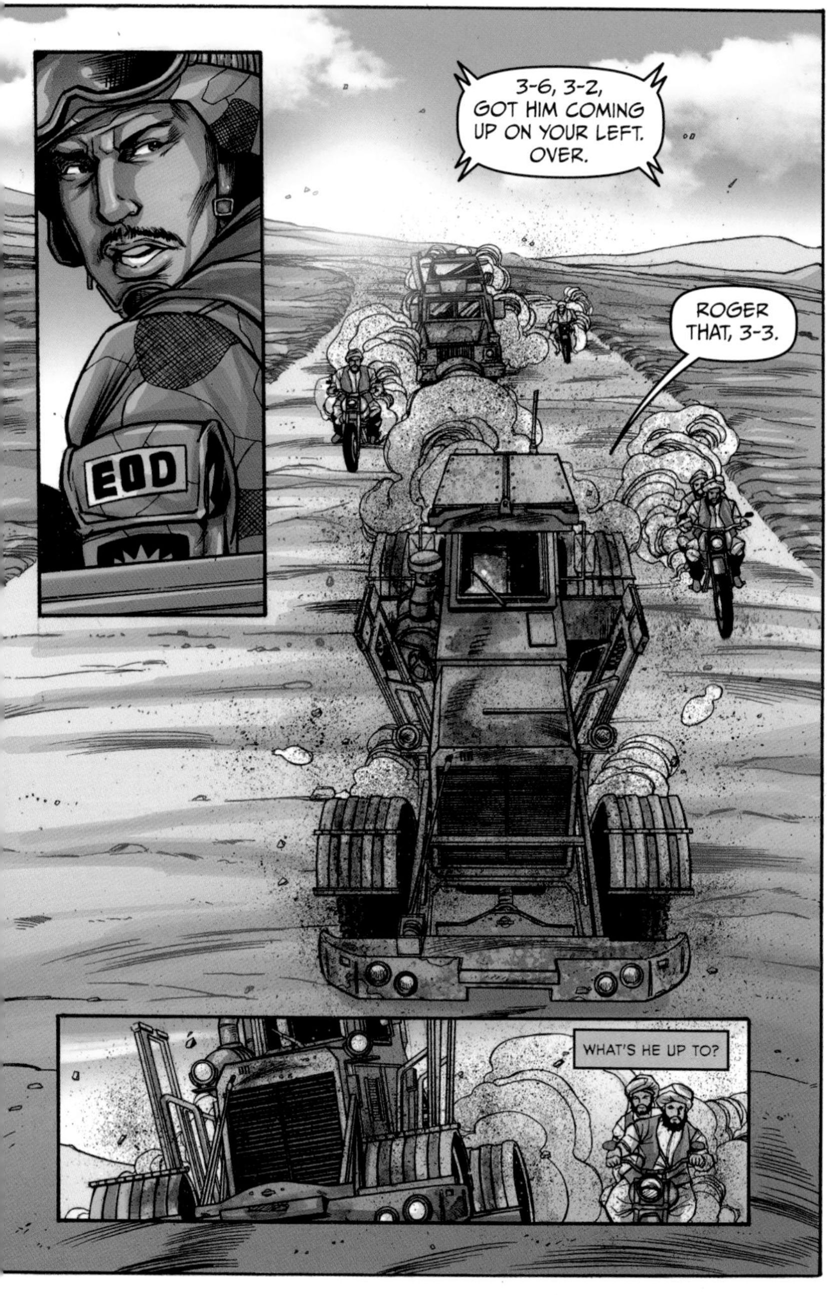

3-6, 3-2, GOT HIM COMING UP ON YOUR LEFT. OVER.
ROGER THAT, 3-3.
EOD
WHAT'S HE UP TO?

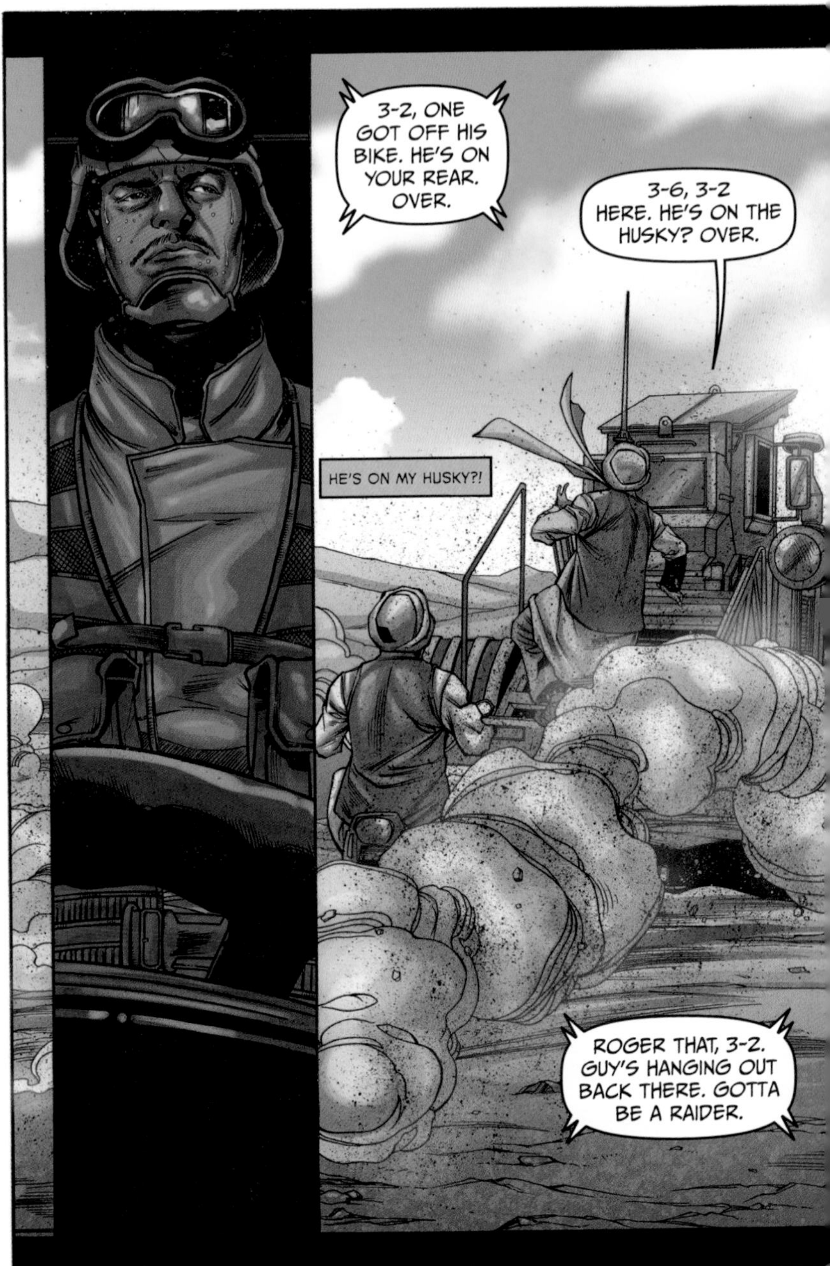
3-2, ONE GOT OFF HIS BIKE. HE'S ON YOUR REAR. OVER.
3-6, 3-2 HERE. HE'S ON THE HUSKY? OVER.
HE'S ON MY HUSKY?!
ROGER THAT, 3-2. GUY'S HANGING OUT BACK THERE. GOTTA BE A RAIDER.

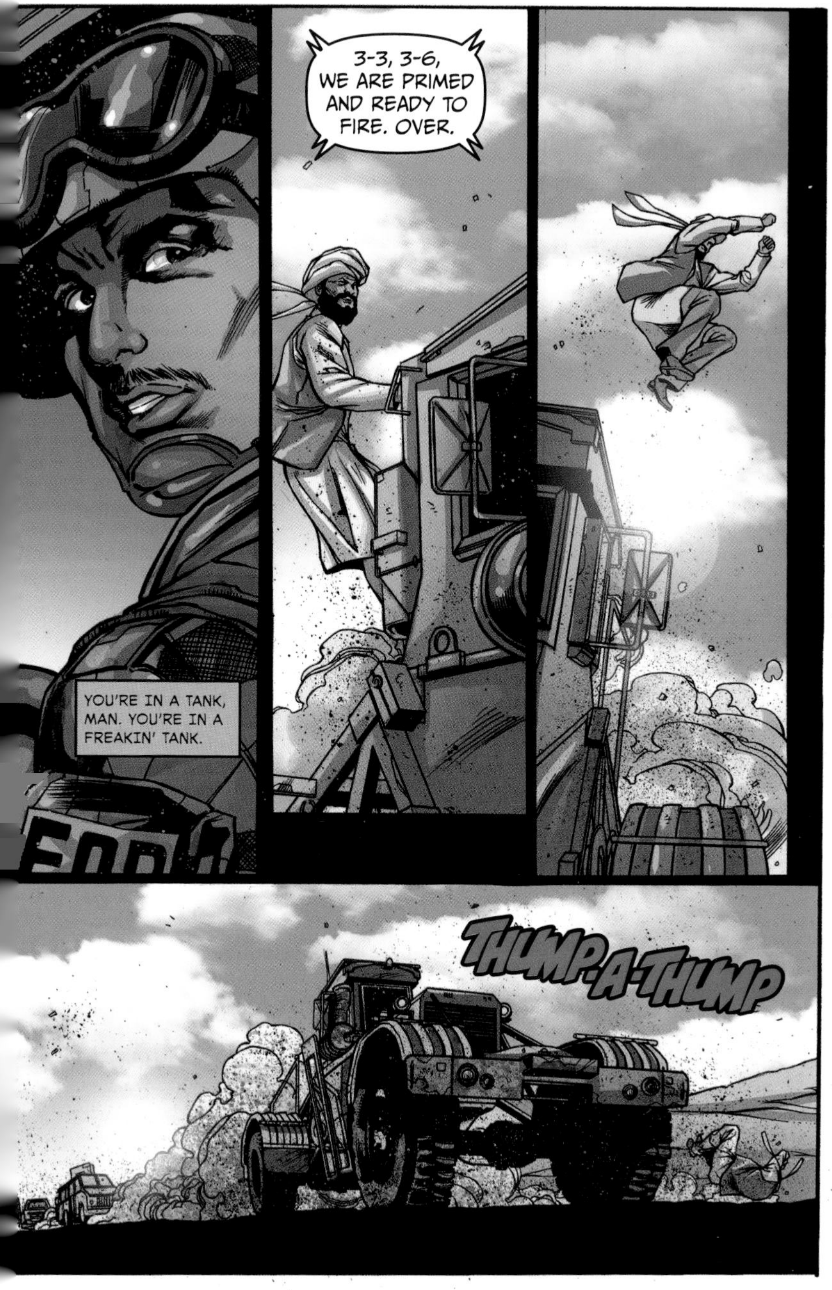
3-3, 3-6, WE ARE PRIMED AND READY TO FIRE. OVER.
YOU'RE IN A TANK, MAN. YOU'RE IN A FREAKIN' TANK.
THUMP-A-THUMP

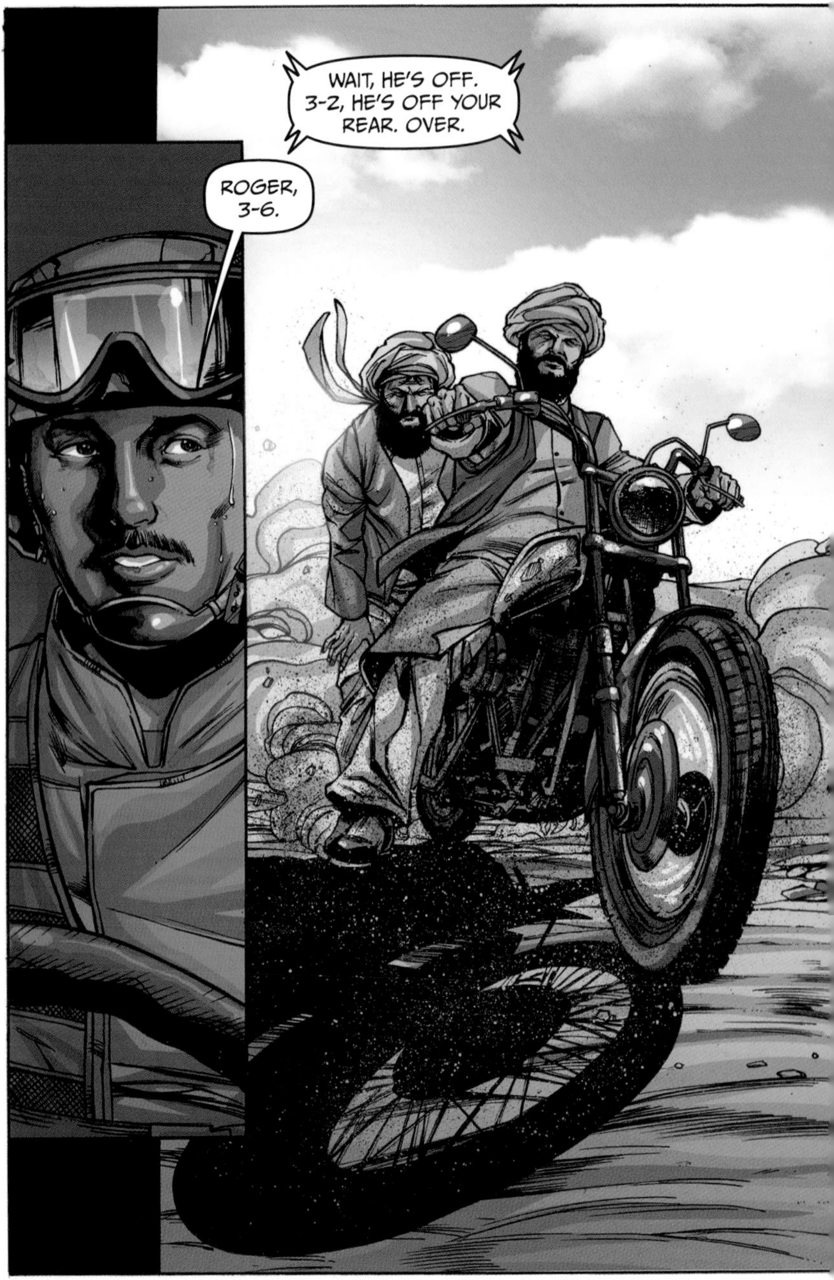
WAIT, HE'S OFF. 3-2, HE'S OFF YOUR REAR. OVER.
ROGER, 3-6.

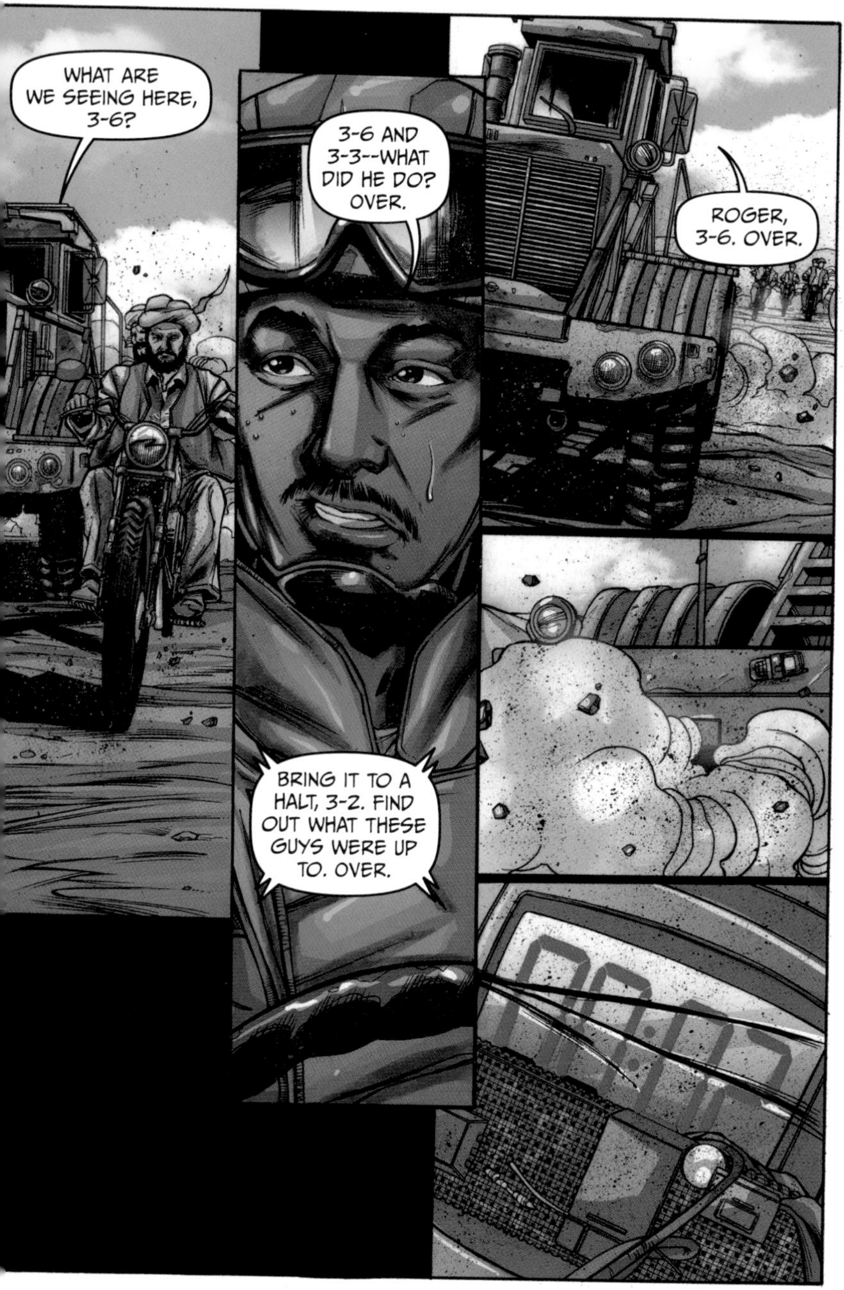
WHAT ARE WE SEEING HERE, 3-6?
3-6 AND 3-3--WHAT DID HE DO? OVER.
ROGER, 3-6. OVER.
BRING IT TO A HALT, 3-2. FIND OUT WHAT THESE GUYS WERE UP TO. OVER.

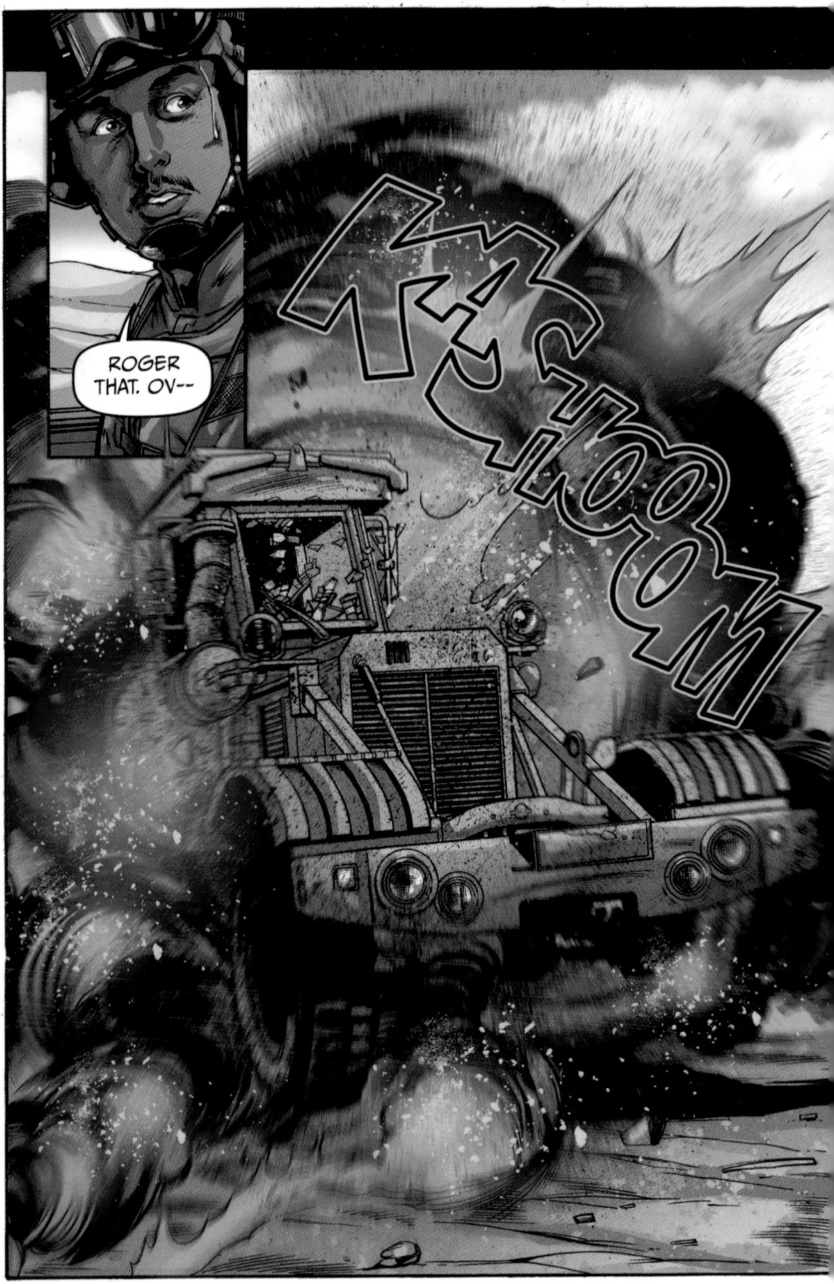
ROGER THAT. OV--
KA-BOOM

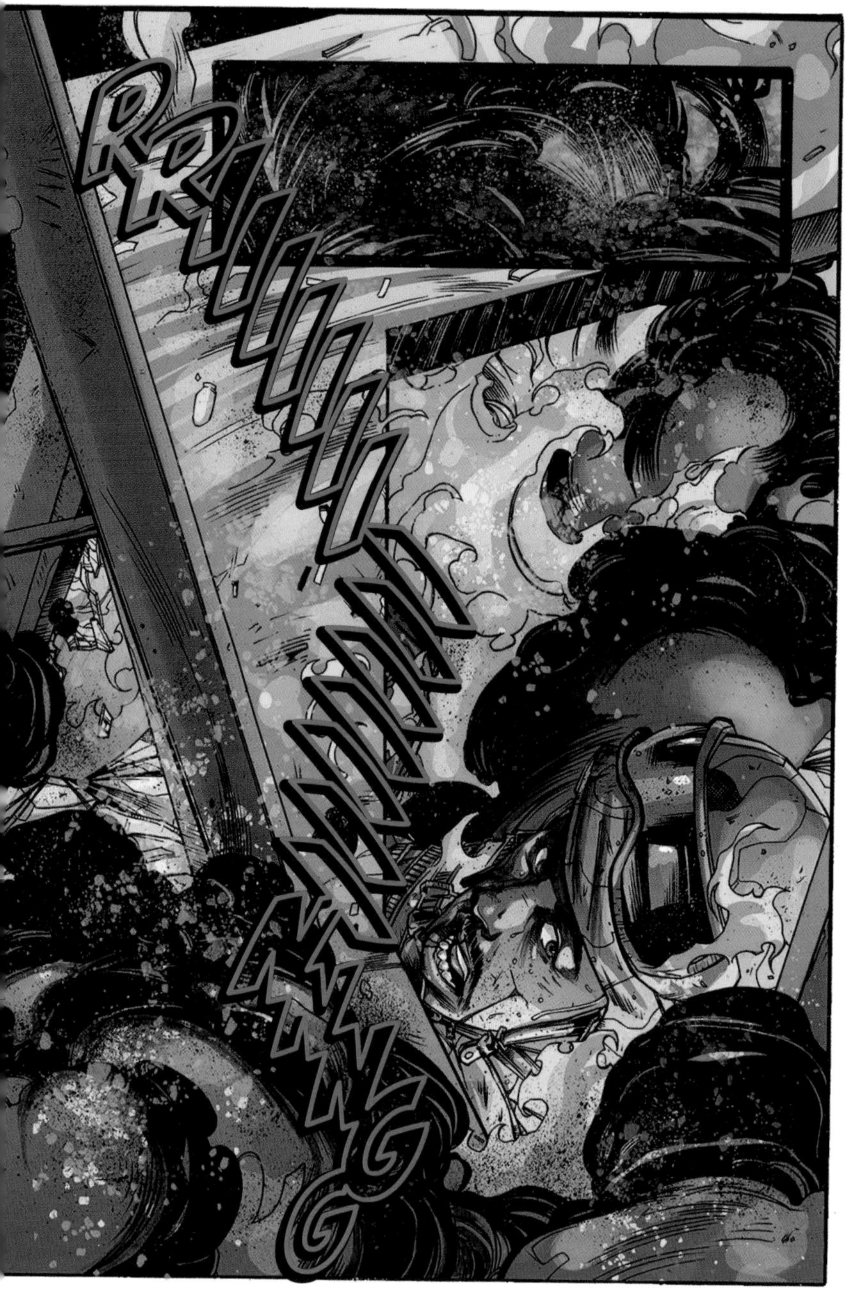
RRIIIIIIIIIINNNGG

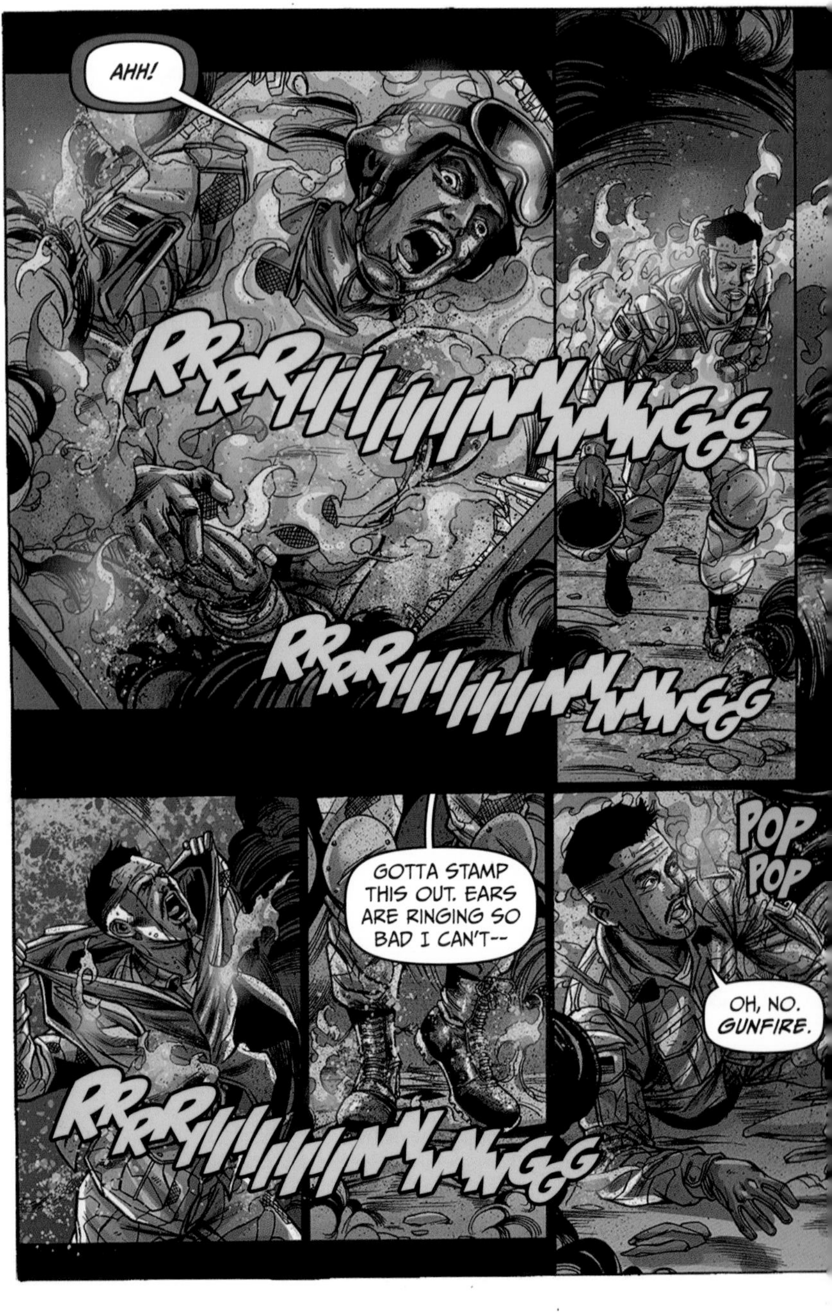
AHH!
RRRRIIIIIIIIINNNNGGG
RRRRIIIIIIIIIINNNNGGG
RRRRIIIIIIIIINNNNGGG
GOTTA STAMP THIS OUT. EARS ARE RINGING SO BAD I CAN'T--
POP POP
OH, NO. GUNFIRE.

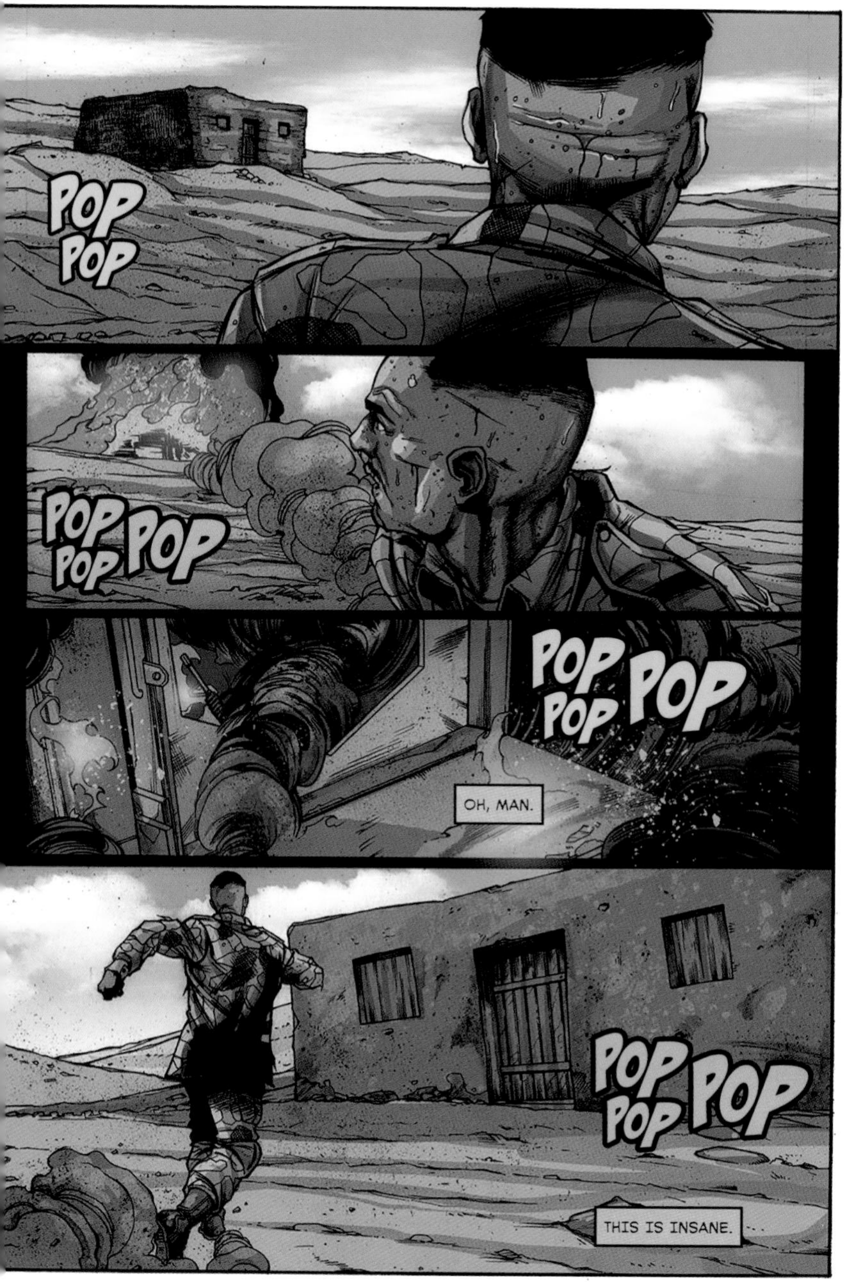
POP
POP
POP
POP POP
POP
POP POP
OH, MAN.
POP
POP POP
THIS IS INSANE.

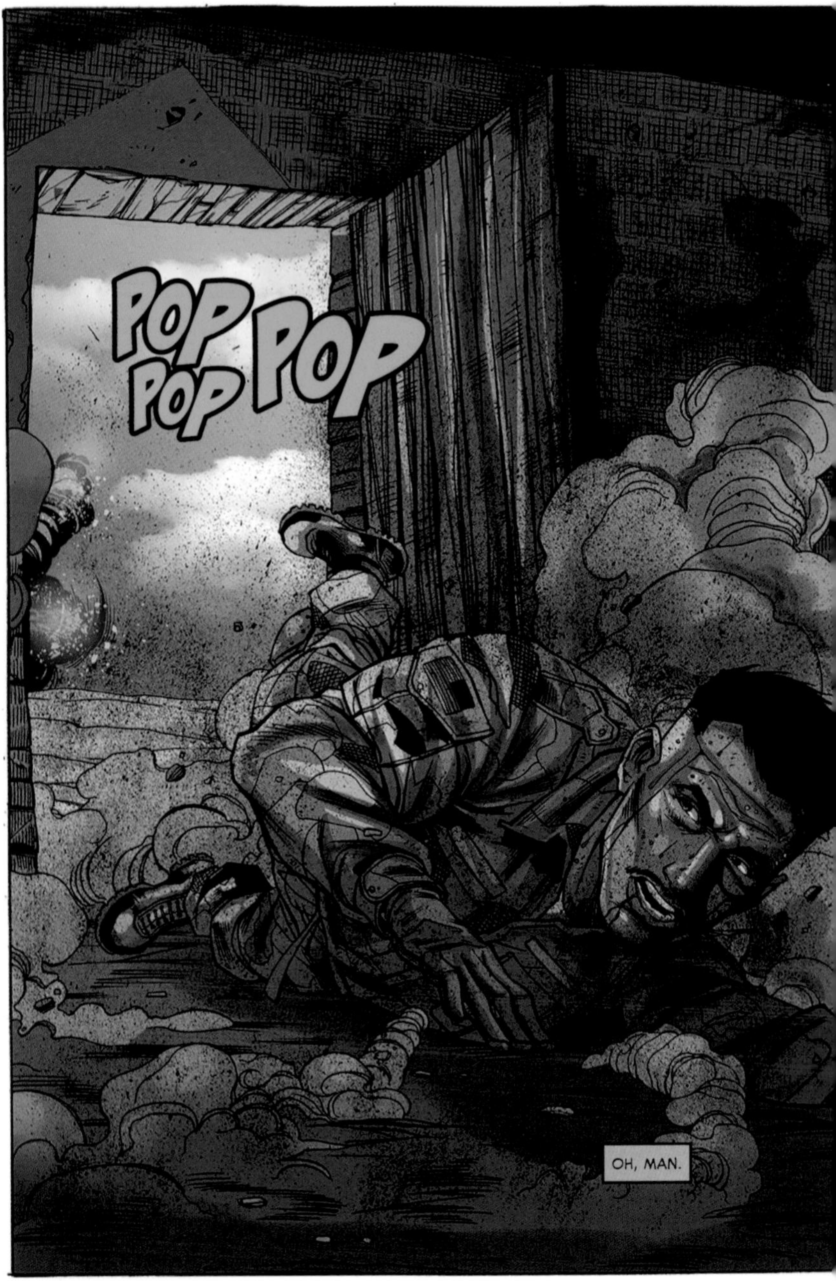
POP
POP POP
OH, MAN.

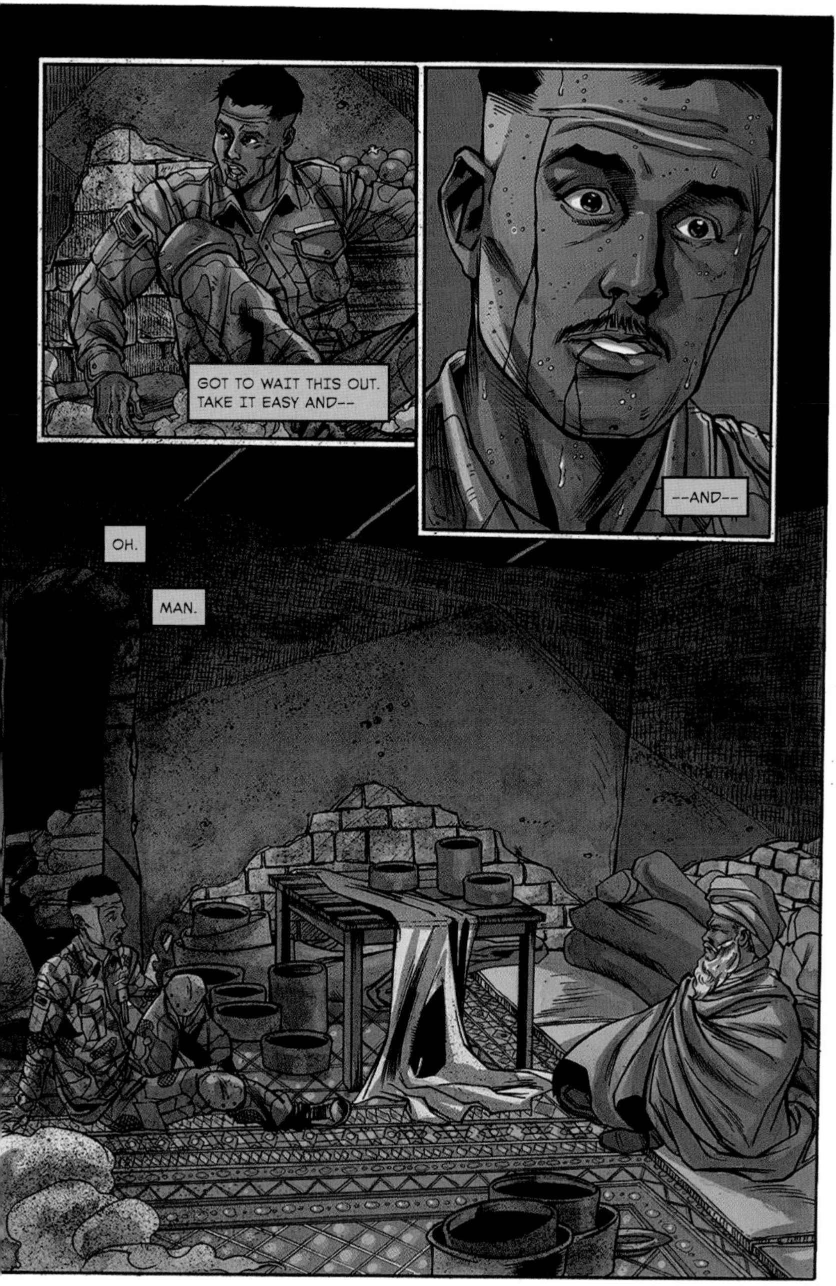
GOT TO WAIT THIS OUT.
TAKE IT EASY AND--
--AND--
OH.
MAN.

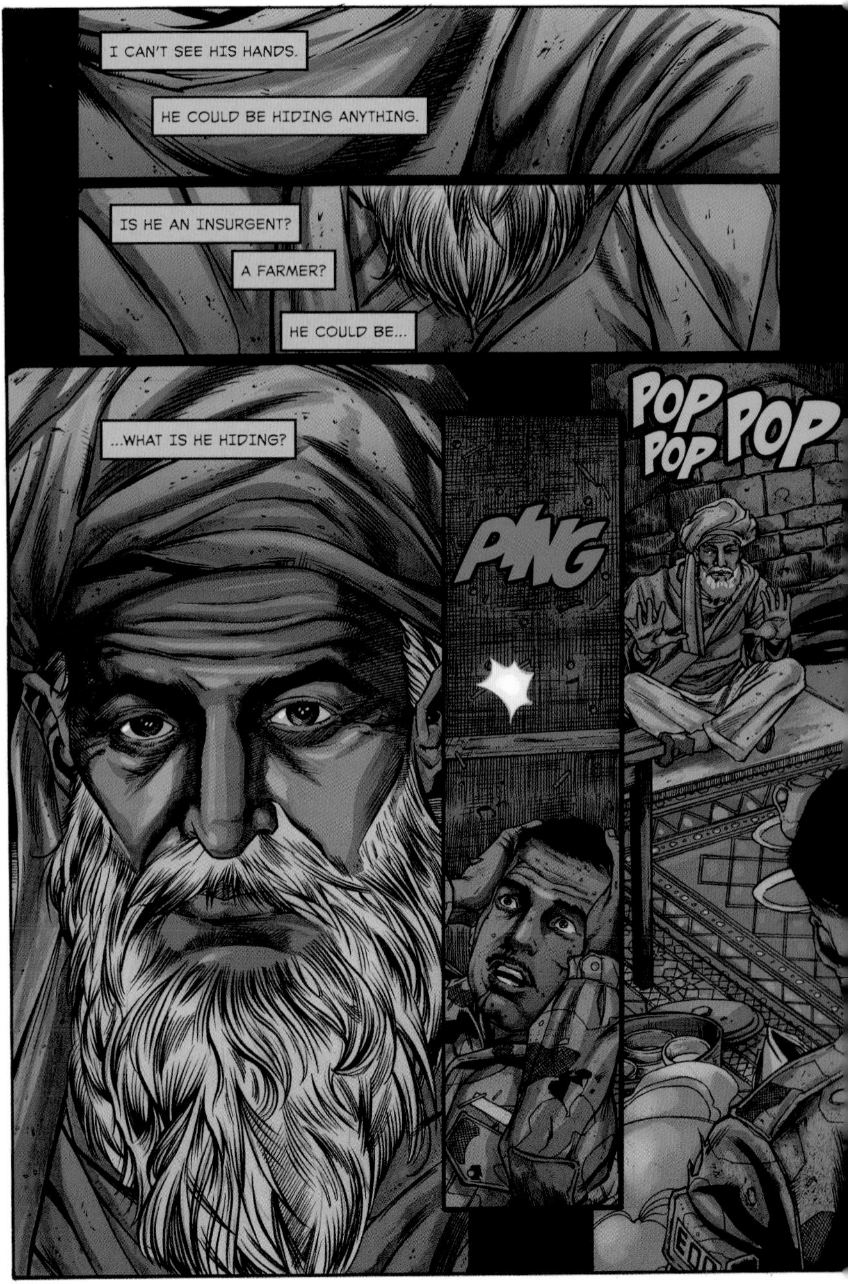
I CAN'T SEE HIS HANDS.
HE COULD BE HIDING ANYTHING.
IS HE AN INSURGENT?
A FARMER?
HE COULD BE...
...WHAT IS HE HIDING?
PING
POP
POP
POP

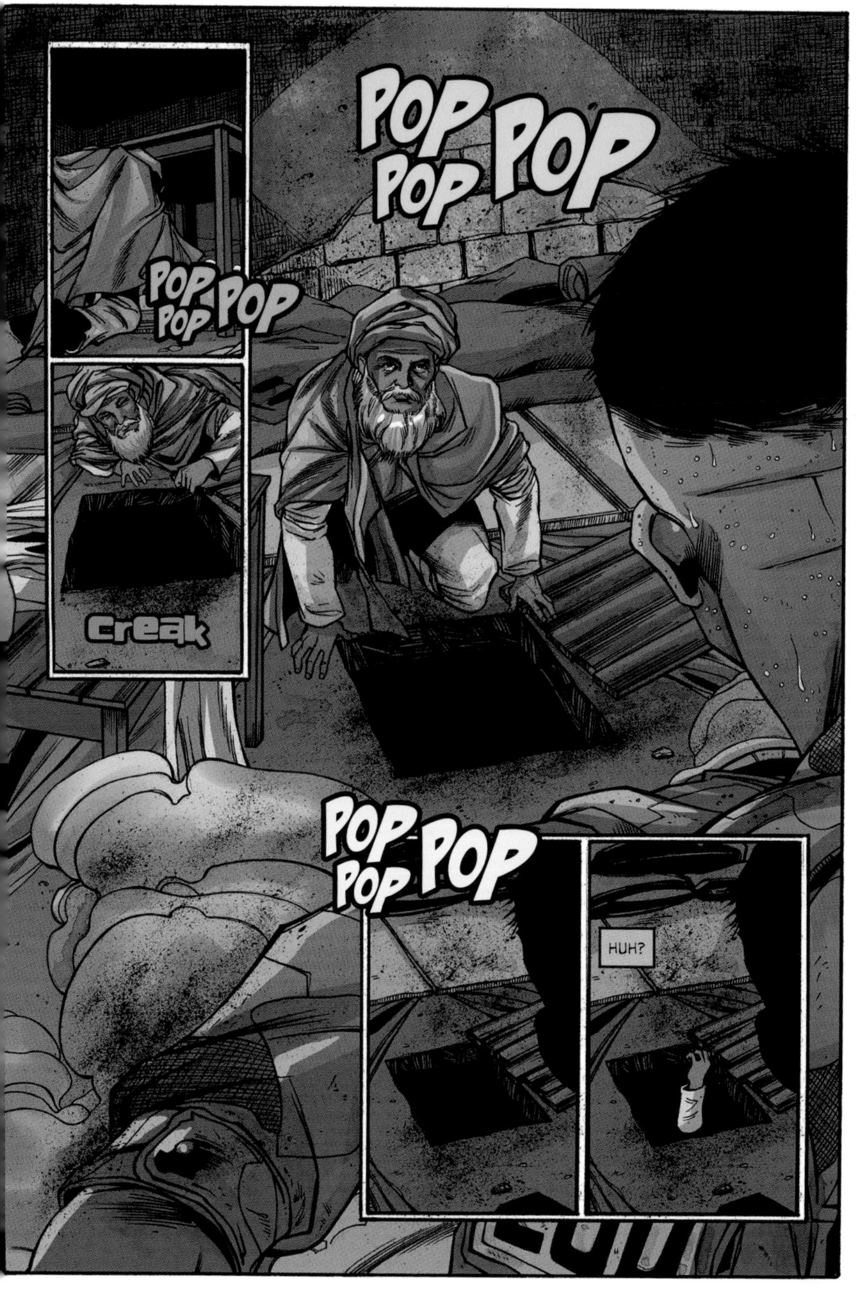
POP POP POP
POP POP POP
Creak
POP POP POP
HUH?

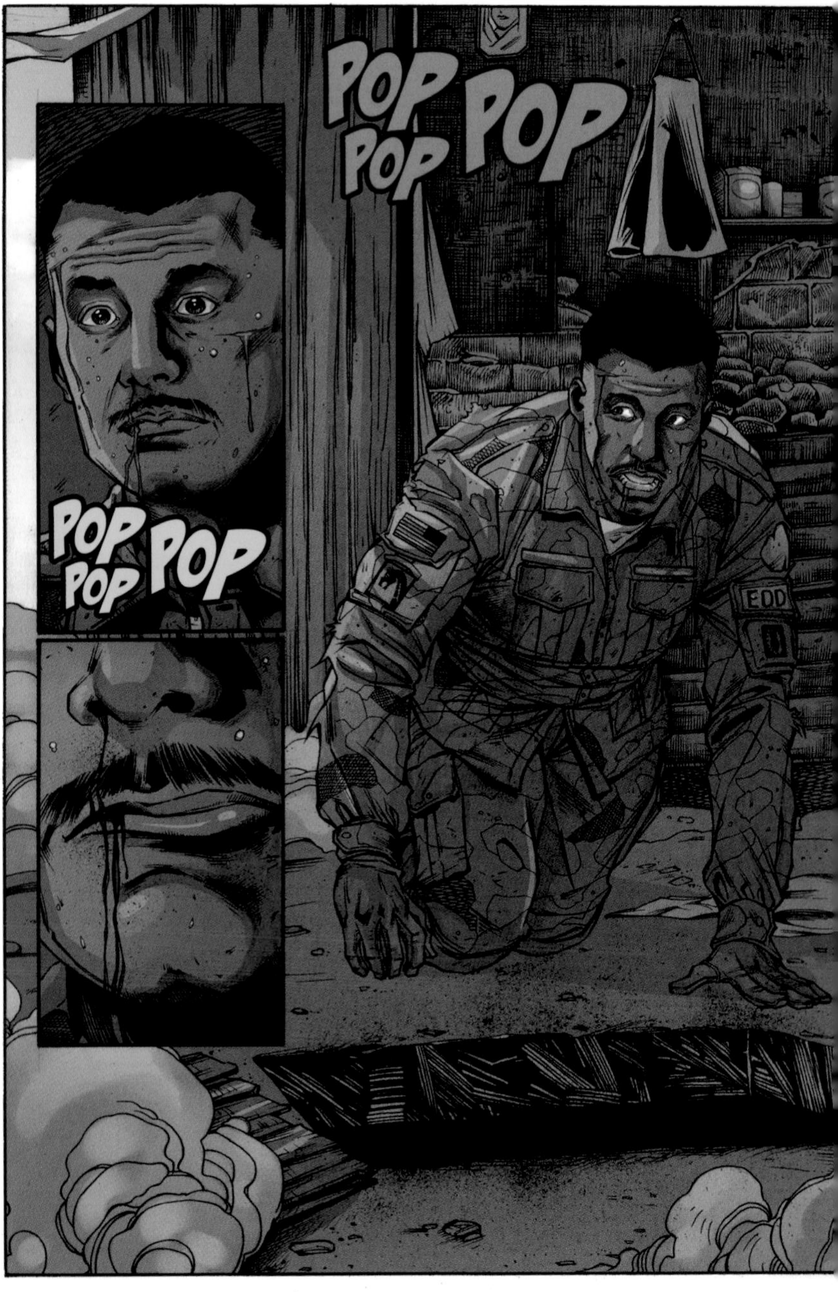
POP POP POP
POP POP POP
EOD

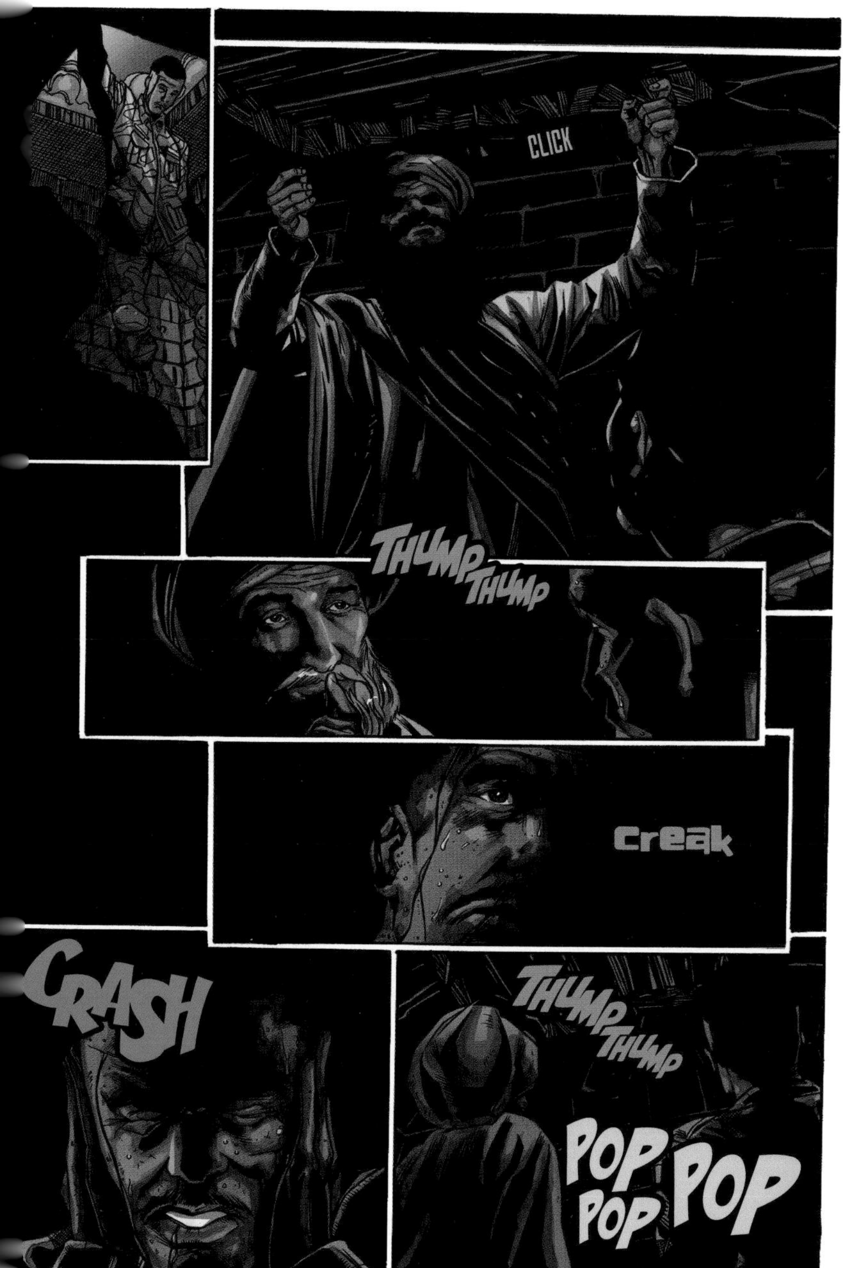
CLICK
THUMP THUMP
Creak
CRASH
THUMP THUMP
POP POP POP

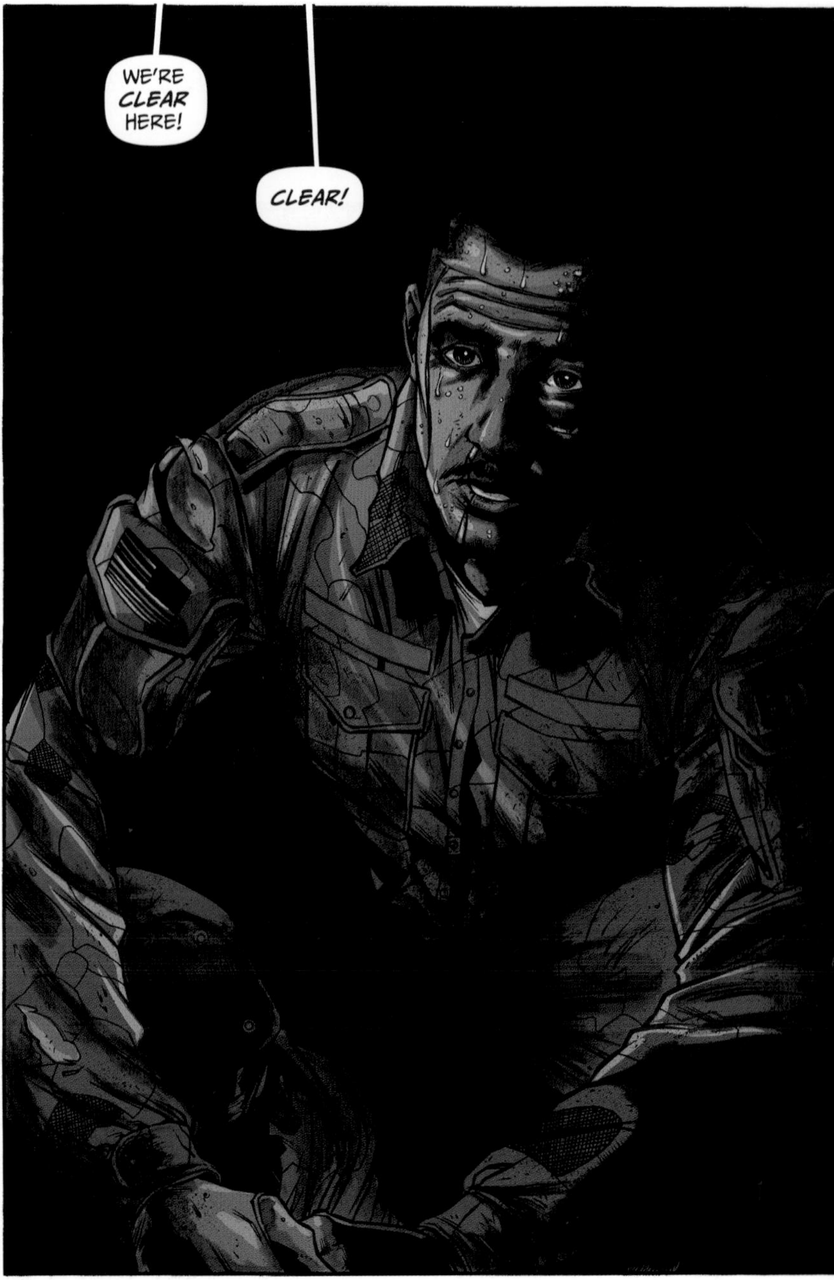
WE'RE CLEAR HERE!
CLEAR!

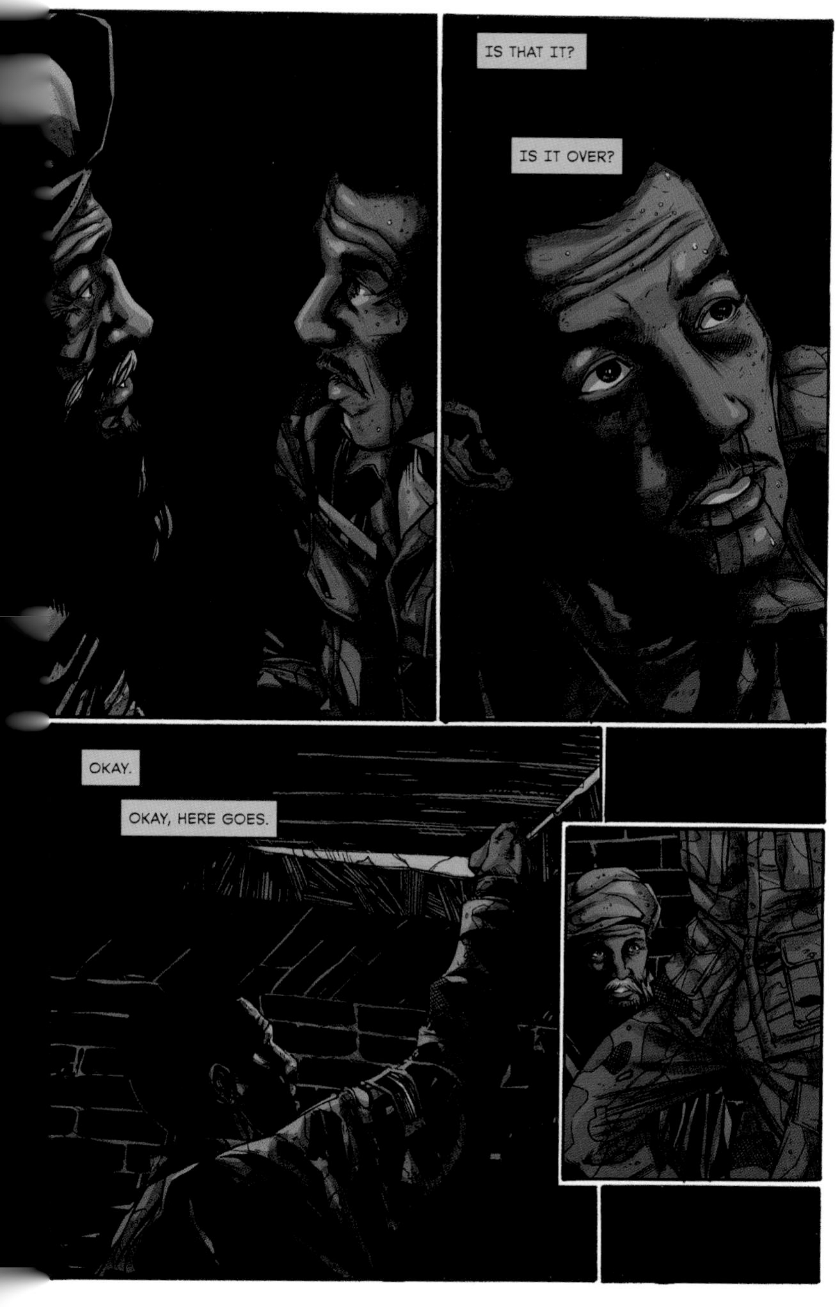
IS THAT IT?
IS IT OVER?
OKAY.
OKAY, HERE GOES.

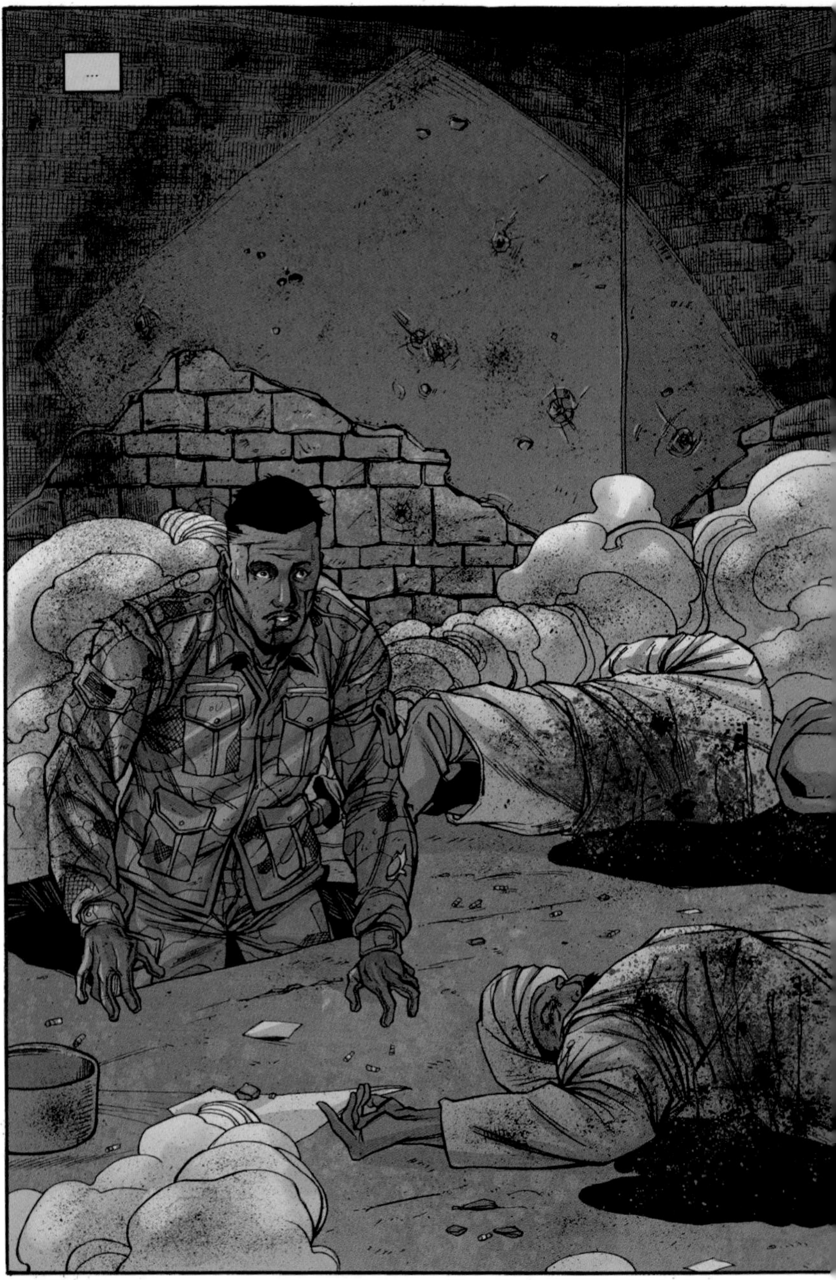
...

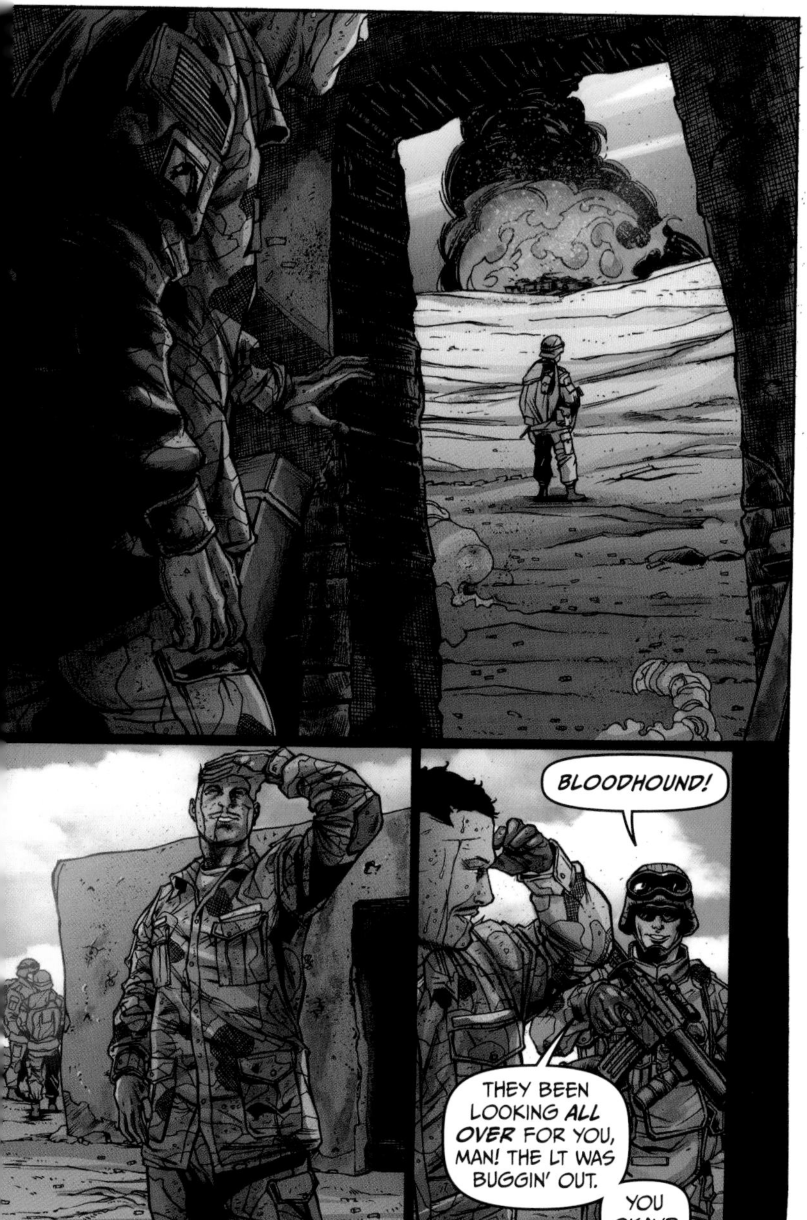
BLOODHOUND!
THEY BEEN LOOKING ALL OVER FOR YOU, MAN! THE LT WAS BUGGIN' OUT.
YOU OKAY?

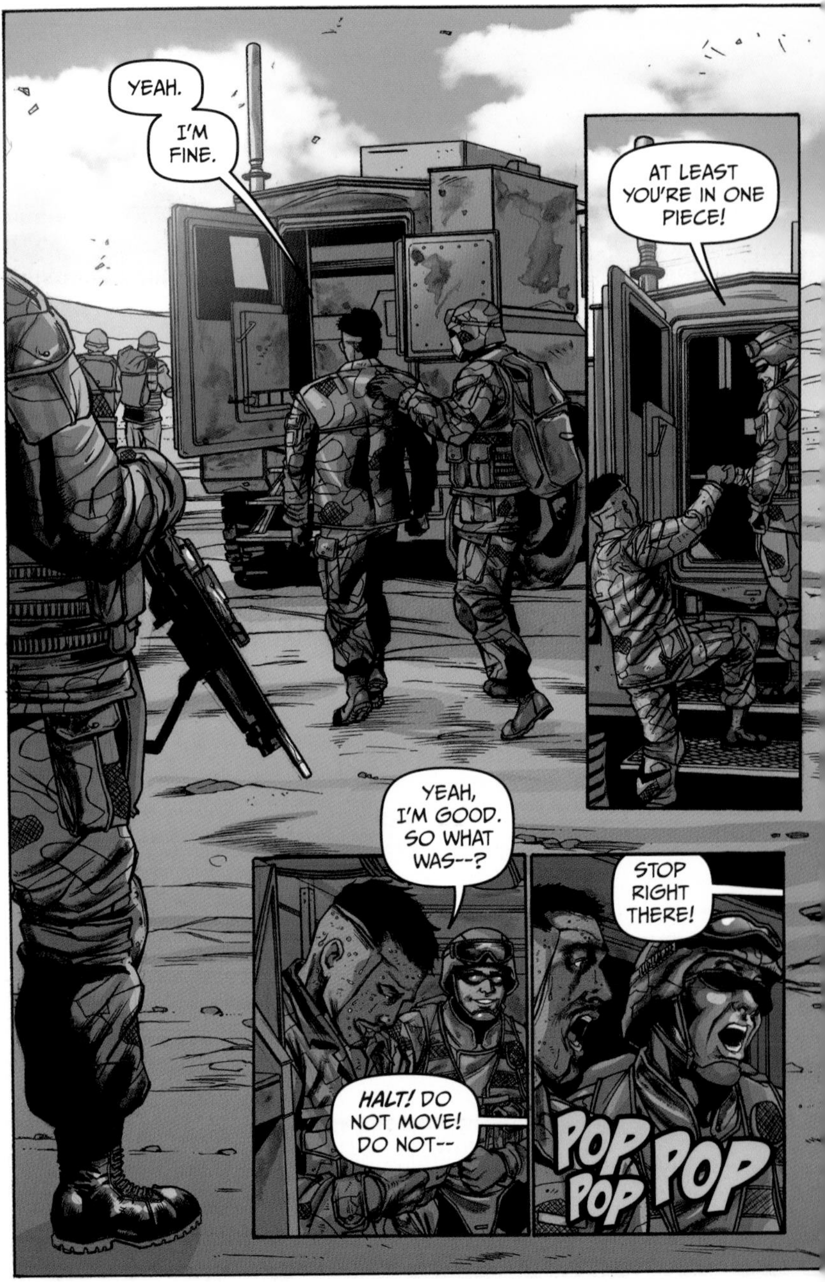
YEAH.
I'M FINE.
AT LEAST YOU'RE IN ONE PIECE!
YEAH, I'M GOOD. SO WHAT WAS--?
STOP RIGHT THERE!
HALT! DO NOT MOVE! DO NOT--
POP POP POP

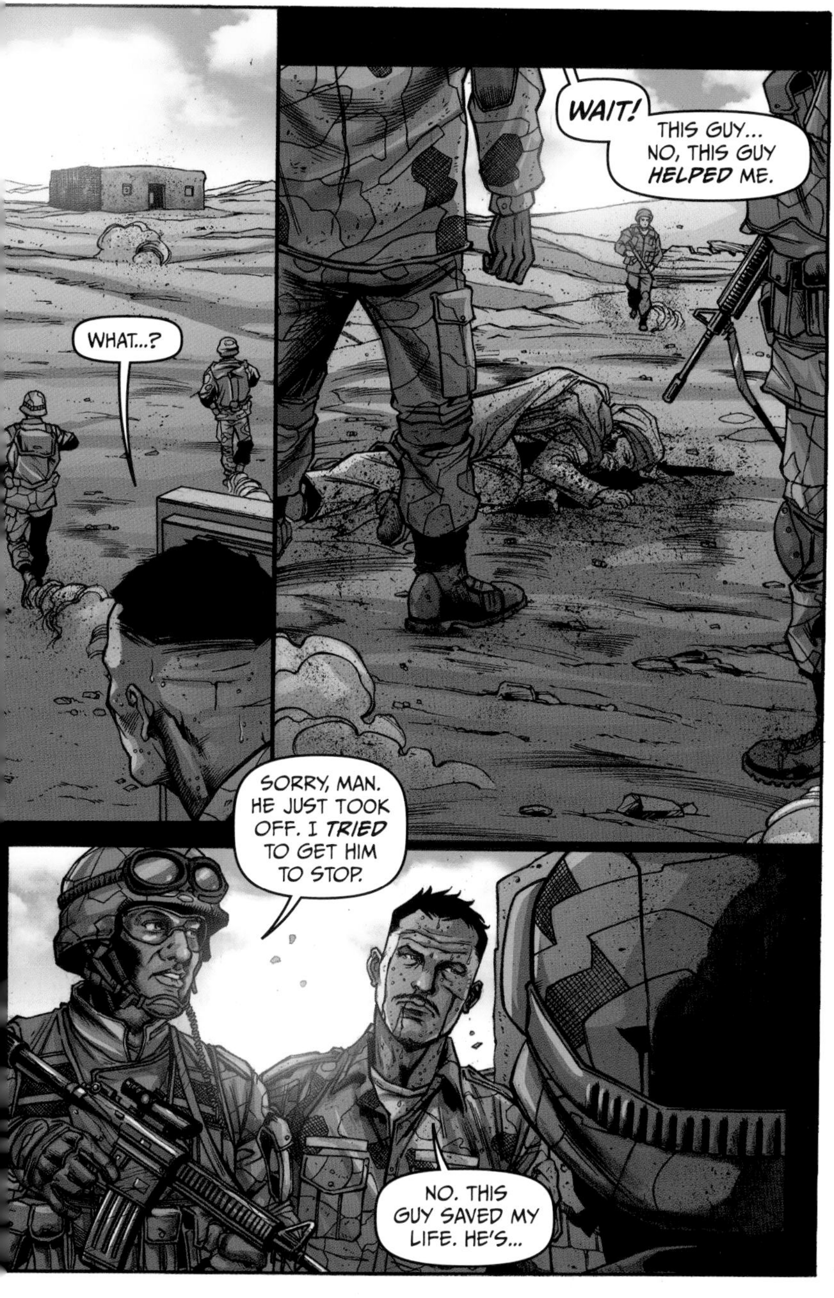
WHAT...?
WAIT!
THIS GUY... NO, THIS GUY HELPED ME.
SORRY, MAN. HE JUST TOOK OFF. I TRIED TO GET HIM TO STOP.
NO. THIS GUY SAVED MY LIFE. HE'S...

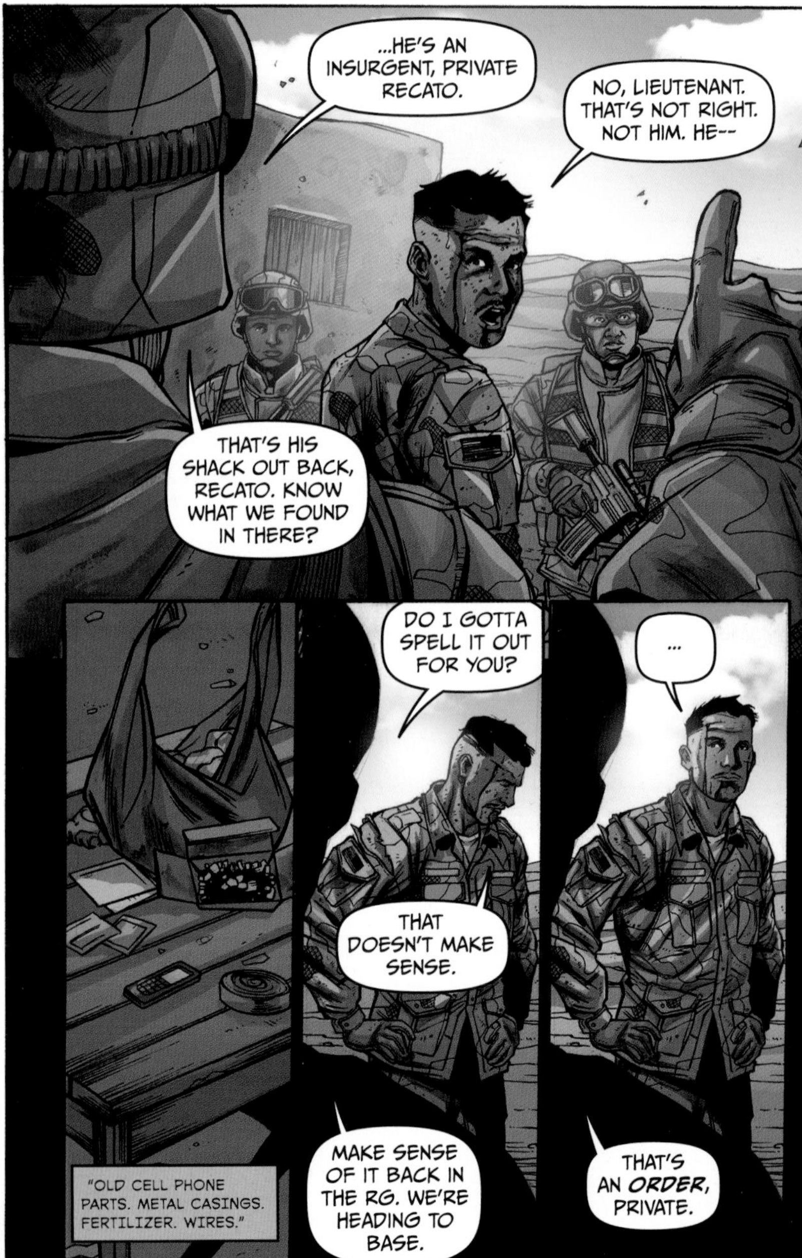

...HE'S AN INSURGENT, PRIVATE RECATO.
NO, LIEUTENANT. THAT'S NOT RIGHT. NOT HIM. HE--
THAT'S HIS SHACK OUT BACK, RECATO. KNOW WHAT WE FOUND IN THERE?
"OLD CELL PHONE PARTS. METAL CASINGS. FERTILIZER. WIRES."
DO I GOTTA SPELL IT OUT FOR YOU?
THAT DOESN'T MAKE SENSE.
MAKE SENSE OF IT BACK IN THE RG. WE'RE HEADING TO BASE.
...
THAT'S AN *ORDER*, PRIVATE.

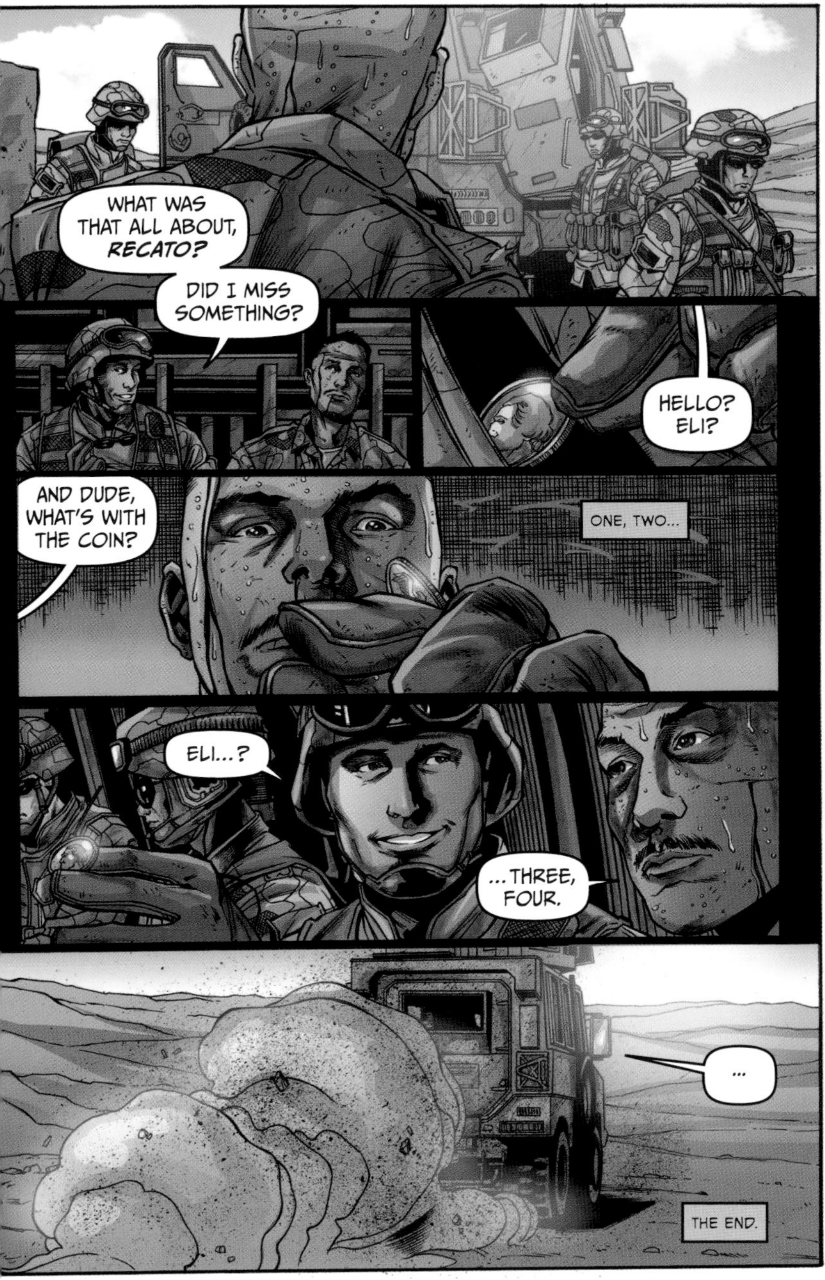
WHAT WAS THAT ALL ABOUT, *RECATO?*
DID I MISS SOMETHING?
HELLO? ELI?
AND DUDE, WHAT'S WITH THE COIN?
ONE, TWO...
ELI...?
...THREE, FOUR.
...
THE END.

EOD SOLDIERS

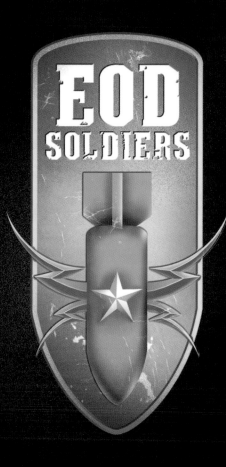

★EOD HISTORY★

Explosive Ordnance Disposal (EOD) soldiers are famous for their heroic work in war zones such as Iraq and Afghanistan. But the history of modern bomb disposal dates back more than 75 years. Early in World War II (1939–1945), the British military faced a growing problem. As German warplanes dropped bombs on British cities, some of the devices hit the ground without exploding. These unexploded bombs were a dangerous mix of duds and live devices with delayed fuses that could explode hours later. At first, the disposal of unexploded bombs fell to untrained British engineers. But high casualties soon led to formal bomb-disposal training in each branch of the British military services.

Halfway around the world, U.S. military officials were watching how the British were handling bomb disposal. They knew that if the United States entered the war, they too would need to deal with unexploded bombs. At first, they thought civilians could be trained for bomb disposal. As a result, the Office of Civilian Defense created the Chemical Warfare School, which included bomb-disposal training. But military officials soon realized that bomb disposal was too dangerous for civilians. By January 1942, both the Army and the Navy established their own schools to formally train soldiers and sailors in bomb disposal.

Both branches of the military continued training their bomb-disposal units separately until 1947. At that time, the Army began sending officers and senior enlisted soldiers to the Navy school, now called the U.S. Navy EOD School. Then in 1951, the Navy took joint responsibility for all EOD training. Today, the Naval School Explosive Ordnance Disposal is located at Eglin Air Force Base in Florida. Volunteers from all branches of the U.S. military attend to learn the life and death skills needed to be EOD soldiers.

VISUAL QUESTIONS

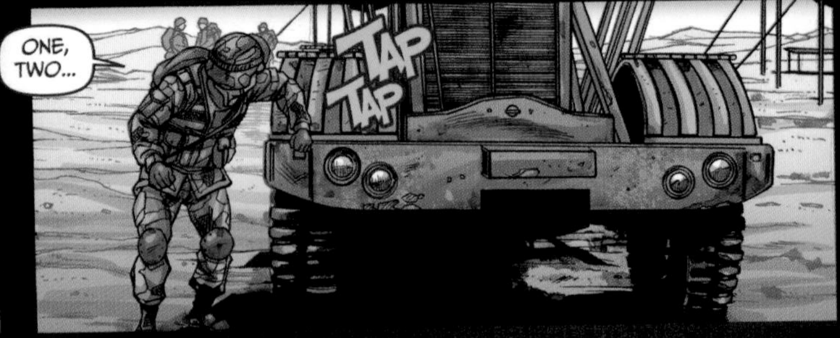
ONE, TWO...
TAP TAP

1. Why do you think Eli taps on the Husky before he begins the mission? What does this behavior tell you about his character?

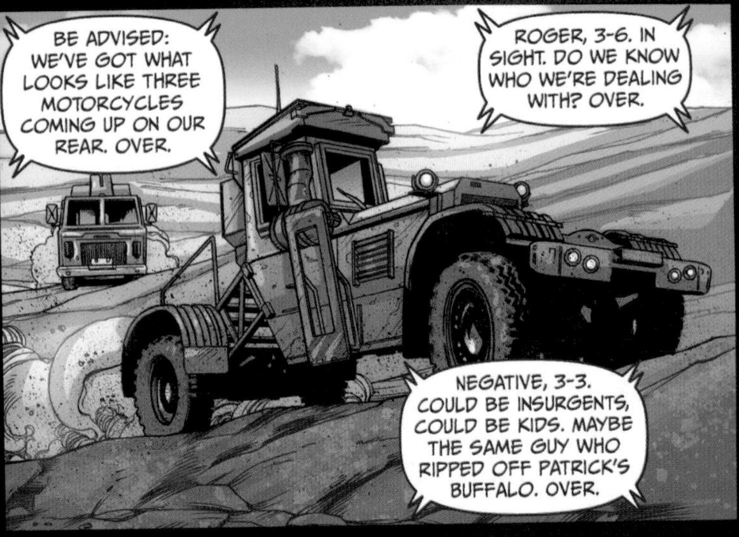
BE ADVISED: WE'VE GOT WHAT LOOKS LIKE THREE MOTORCYCLES COMING UP ON OUR REAR. OVER.
ROGER, 3-6. IN SIGHT. DO WE KNOW WHO WE'RE DEALING WITH? OVER.
NEGATIVE, 3-3. COULD BE INSURGENTS, COULD BE KIDS. MAYBE THE SAME GUY WHO RIPPED OFF PATRICK'S BUFFALO. OVER.

2. Eli's team members have a conversation in this panel. How does the style of the bubbles help you understand how the conversation is possible?

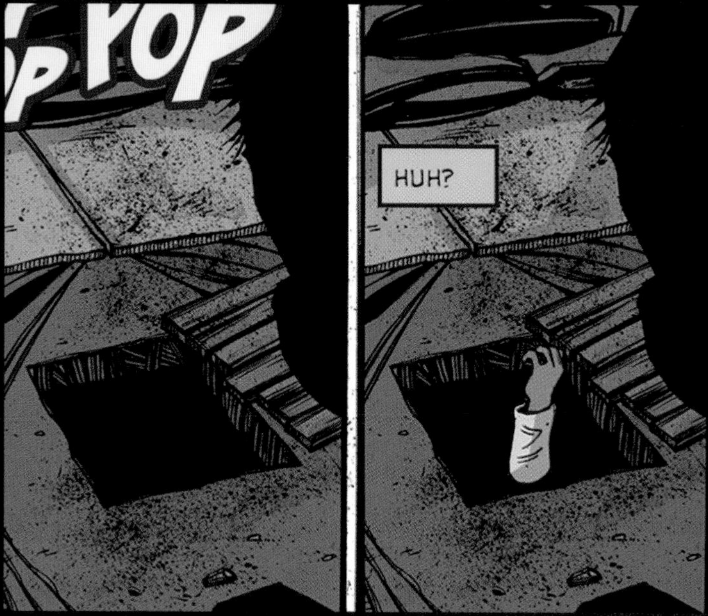
P YOP
HUH?

3. These two panels are almost identical. What do the small differences between them tell you about what Eli is thinking and feeling at this moment? How do you know?

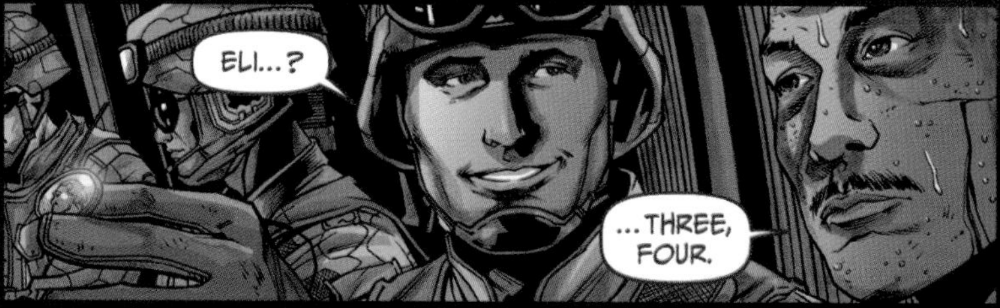
ELI...?
...THREE, FOUR.

4. Why does Eli start turning his coin and counting again at the end of the story? How does he feel? What details in the art help you know?

AUTHOR

Matthew K. Manning is the author of more than 40 books and dozens of comic books. His work ranges from the Amazon top-selling hardcover, *Batman: A Visual History*, to the children's book, *Superman: An Origin Story*, to a series of graphic novels featuring the military's bomb squad in Afghanistan. Over the course of his career, he has written books starring Batman, Superman, Spider-Man, Wolverine, the Joker, *Scooby-Doo*, Iron Man, Wonder Woman, Flash, Thor, Green Lantern, Captain America, the Hulk, Harley Quinn, and the Avengers. Currently one of the regular writers for IDW's comic series, *Teenage Mutant Ninja Turtles: Amazing Adventures*, Manning has also written for several other comic book titles, including serving as one of the regular writers for *Beware the Batman*, *The Batman Strikes!*, *Legion of Super-Heroes in the 31st Century*, and *Teenage Mutant Ninja Turtles: New Animated Adventures*. He lives in Asheville, North Carolina, with his wife, Dorothy, and his two daughters, Lillian and Gwendolyn.

GLOSSARY

Buffalo (BUHF-uh-loh)—an armored military vehicle with six wheels that is mine-resistant and ambush-protected

casing (kayss-ING)—an empty shell from a fired bullet

casualty (KAZH-oo-uhl-tee)—someone who is injured, captured, killed, or missing in an accident, a disaster, or a war

civilian (si-VIL-yuhn)—a person who is not in the military

fertilizer (FUHR-tuh-ly-zuhr)—a substance added to soil to make crops grow better; fertilizer is sometimes used as an ingredient in IEDs and other homemade bombs

IED (EYE-ee-dee)—stands for improvised explosive device; a homemade bomb often made with material not usually found in bombs

insurgent (in-SUR-juhnt)—a person who rebels and fights against his or her country's ruling government and those who support it

LT (EL-tee)—stands for lieutenant; a rank in the U.S. military above sergeant and below captain

modesty (MOD-eh-stee)—the quality of being without vanity or boastfulness

private (PRYE-vit)—a soldier of lowest rank in the military

RG (AR-gee)—a lightly armored military transport vehicle that is mine-resistant

steer (STEER)—to guide or direct

MORE EOD SOLDIERS

EOD
TWO SIDES
MANNING
FURUZONO
LIMA

EOD
THE MIST
MANNING
FURUZONO
LIMA

EOD
THE LIST
MANNING
FURUZONO
LIMA

EOD
GO SLOW
MANNING
FURUZONO
LIMA

Find cool websites and more books
like this one at www.facthound.com

Just type in the Book ID:
9781496531070
and you are ready to go!

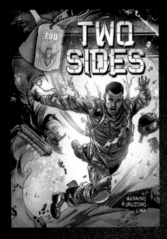